'Have you ever spent the night on a mountainside before?' Max queried.

'Yes, I have,' George responded promptly. 'I've had plenty of survival training.'

'Training exercises.' Max sounded dubious. 'Have you ever spent a night in the open in weather like this? In a situation that involves a real patient?'

George shook her head in exasperation. 'Let's discuss this later, shall we?'

What would Max say if he knew that the only time she had been caught in the open in a situation involving a patient she had *been* the patient? George knew exactly what Max would say. He would be delighted to remind her just how often he had protested that the career she had dreamed about was far too dangerous for anyone, but particularly for a woman. Well, George wasn't going to give him the satisfaction of being able to say I told you so.

Alison Roberts was born in New Zealand and she says, 'I lived in London and Washington DC as a child, and began my working career as a primary school teacher. A lifelong interest in medicine was fostered by my doctor and nurse parents, flatting with doctors and physiotherapists on leaving home, and marriage to a house surgeon who is now a cardiologist. I have also worked as a cardiology technician and research assistant. My husband's medical career took us to Glasgow for two years, which was an ideal place and time to start my writing career. I now live in Christchurch, New Zealand, with my husband, daughter and various pets.'

Recent titles by the same author:

EMOTIONAL RESCUE
NURSE IN NEED

DOCTOR IN DANGER

BY
ALISON ROBERTS

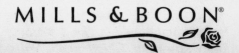

MILLS & BOON®

MILLS & BOON and
MILLS & BOON with the Rose Device
are registered trademarks of the publisher.

First published in Great Britain 2001
Large Print edition 2002
Harlequin Mills & Boon Limited,
Eton House, 18-24 Paradise Road,
Richmond, Surrey TW9 1SR

© Alison Roberts 2001

ISBN 0 263 17180 9

Set in Times Roman 16½ on 18 pt.
17-0702-51973

Printed and bound in Great Britain
by Antony Rowe Ltd, Chippenham, Wiltshire

CHAPTER ONE

'JUST like new.' Pilot Ted Scott stepped back and eyed the gleaming canary yellow metal with satisfaction.

He stuffed the polishing cloth he had been using into the pocket of his overalls and turned away from the machine. The post-mission check and clean-up were now complete. A glance at his watch confirmed Ted's suspicion that it was nearly time to fire up the small tractor and drag the mobile pad and the large helicopter it supported back into the hangar for the night. Ted moved towards the fuel tank to rewind the hose, scanning the interior of the cavernous hangar as he did so. No sign of any movement in there so the staff meeting hadn't finished yet.

Ted latched the pump nozzle back into place and noted the change in the gauge figures. Also satisfying. They had all earned their keep today. Three rescue missions and they had all gone without a hitch, which was exactly the way Ted Scott liked them. The MVA on the northern motorway had been a big job with two seriously injured victims to transport. The premature twins from a remote country hospital had needed a lot of organisation with incubators and extra medical staff for their emergency evacuation, but the broken wrist from the nearby Mount Hutt ski field had been a piece of cake despite the pick-up of the nor-westerly breeze and had been a good way to finish a busy day.

The vibration from the tractor engine almost disguised the fact that Ted's pager was going off. He unclipped it from his top pocket with some dismay. The feeling increased as he read the message to stand by for a rescue mission.

'Sector 7,' Ted muttered. 'Top of the bloody mountains, that's where it'll be.' He shook his head. It could take them an hour to get there and locate their target and the weather could be marginal. A nor'-wester on this side of the Alps meant foul weather on the other side. And Sector 7 straddled both sides. Remaining daylight could present another challenge. Ted coded the automatic dialing system in his cellphone to give him the meteorological office.

An update on weather conditions was his first priority. Then he would go and find out the details of the mission. Thoughts of going home had already evaporated. Somebody needed their help. Someone's life might depend on it and that, after all, was what this job was all about.

The strident beeping of two separate pagers had broken the silence around the long table in the staffroom. The group of paramedics looked towards the sound.

'Saved by the bell, Mozzie,' someone commented wryly.

'Are you kidding?' Murray Peters pushed his chair back and stood up as he scanned his pager. 'Another job's the last thing I need right now.' He sighed heavily. 'Not Sector 7,' he muttered. 'Please!' With a resigned expression, Murray moved towards the telephone that linked the base directly to the emergency services communications centre.

The man at the head of the table, Phil Warrington, also pushed his chair back. 'Time we packed up, anyway. You've all got plenty to think about and we won't proceed without further discussion.'

There was a general shuffling as the group broke up.

'Don't forget the twentieth of next month,' Phil added. 'That's my official farewell bash. Barbecue. Bring your own meat but the drinks will be on the house.'

'I'll check my diary.' Mike Bingham eased his tall and very lean frame into a standing position.

'You'll be the first in line, Stretch,' Harry Greene declared with a grin. 'I've never known you to pass on a free drink.'

'Pass out more like it,' Ross White added.

Mike had opened his diary.

'Who's on duty on the twentieth?' Harry queried.

'Mozzie and Big George,' Mike reported.

'Oh, hard luck, George.' The men turned to the other end of the table but the object of their sympathy was busy watching Murray's end of the telephone conversation and just grinned and shrugged in acknowledgement. Judging by the scrutiny and finger-tracing of the large wall map beside the desk, arrangements for the late mission were being confirmed.

Georgina Collins closed her notebook and rose to her feet. Even with the extra inch that the heeled, army-issue-style boots she was wearing gave her, the height of five feet four inches she commanded was anything but big. The slender frame inside the fluorescent orange overalls added to the affectionate mockery her nickname bestowed. George was tiny but there wasn't a man present in this room that didn't respect her strength, determination or skill. George had earned her stripes and the disappointment that she wouldn't make the barbecue party was genuine.

'Throw a sickie, George,' Mike suggested.

'Are you going to stand in for her, then, Stretch?'

Before Mike could answer, Ted Scott entered the staffroom.

'What's the forecast, Red?' Harry queried.

Ted shook his head. 'Marginal. Won't really know until we get there.' He joined George at the end of the table. 'Are we still on, then?'

'Let's find out.' They both moved to join Murray at the main desk. He replaced the receiver.

'We're on,' he reported glumly. 'Target's somewhere on the descent from Minchin Pass down Townsend Creek.' Murray turned to a rack of maps and flipped the sections. He withdrew a much more detailed map of the area they would be heading towards, located the track and followed it with his finger. 'They were heading for Locke Hut on the Taramakau River. They left the pass about an hour and a half ago so they should be about halfway down the descent.'

'That's steep,' Ted commented.

'And miles from anywhere,' Murray nodded. 'It would take at least six hours for a ground crew to get in from the main road at Aickens which would be the nearest entrance point to the park.'

'They would have to pick one of the longest tramping routes in the Arthur's Pass National Park,' George said dryly. 'Do you know what's happened precisely?'

Murray nodded. 'There's two trampers. They were negotiating the bushed terraces on the left side rather than scrambling over the boulders of the creek bed. One of them has fallen down a bank approximately ten metres.

He landed in the creek, on the boulders, and was apparently KO'd for two to three minutes, but there's no indication of serious head injury at this stage. He's got bruised ribs and one moderate laceration to his left forearm, but the main problem at this stage is a compound tib and fib. He's lost an estimated 750 mils of blood.'

'Compound fracture?' George echoed. 'Seven-fifty mils? That's fairly precise.' She frowned. 'Does one of the trampers happen to be an orthopaedic surgeon by some chance?'

'Close.' Murray's smile was wry. 'The injured man is one of the emergency department consultants—Dougal Donaldson. Do you know him?'

'By sight.' George nodded. 'He hasn't been there very long. Three months at most.' Dougal was a Scot. Enthusiastic, good-looking and already very popular. But George had avoided him like the plague. She had an aversion to all things Scottish and she was probably the only female in Dougal's new orbit that didn't find his broad Glaswegian accent remotely attractive.

'I guess there's no chance of it not being a winching job, then.' George followed Ted and Murray who were now moving through the empty hangar towards the supplies room.

'Nope.' Murray looked at his watch and sighed.

George smiled. 'It's your turn to dangle, mate,' she told Murray.

'No way!'

'Toss a coin?' George was teasing her colleague.

'Come on, George. You know it's Sophie's birthday party tonight. She's sixteen. I can't miss it. If I get left on the top of a bloody mountain for the night she'll never forgive me.'

'How likely is that?' George countered. 'We'll be in and out in no time flat. You'll be home by 8.30.'

'Did you say there were two trampers?' Ted broke in. 'Are we going to winch them both?'

'Depends how we go for time and what the weather's like. Dougal's mate's not injured. He could walk out with the gear tomorrow. Search and Rescue might send a ground team in to meet him.'

'Who is he? Another doctor?' George had taken the winch harness from its hook and was stepping into it. Murray gave her a grateful smile as he collected packs of equipment.

'Don't know. He's not local. Apparently he described himself as a friend. His name's John. Actually, I'm not sure if it was him who made the emergency cellphone call or whether it was Dougal. The batteries ran out before they finished the call.'

The team was now moving from the supplies room towards the helicopter. Other staff, still dispersing from the staff meeting, joined them as they crossed the hangar again.

'What would you have said, Mozzie?' Ross queried. 'If you'd had a chance to answer the question Phil asked in the meeting?'

'About what, Snow?' Murray's thoughts were already focused on their mission.

'The idea of having a doctor permanently on base.'

Murray grunted noncommittally. 'I'll have to give it some thought.'

'What do you reckon, George?' Ross asked seriously.

'I don't like the idea.' George paused, adjusting the heavy harness straps on her shoulders. Murray and Ted carried on towards the helicopter pad. 'It'll mean they drop paramedic staff numbers so some of us would be out of a job.'

'Sounds like they want you somewhere else anyway,' Ross said cautiously. 'What was Phil's comment about seeing you behind his desk all about?'

George sighed. 'I've been offered the position of Operations Supervisor again. I'm not really interested. It's a desk job predominantly, even though I'd still get the occasional mission. But although I realise it's actually a promotion, I'm not quite ready to be put out to pasture yet, despite what many people thought a while ago.'

Ross nodded sympathetically, then frowned with concern. 'How *is* the back these days, George?'

'Fine, thanks.' George brushed the query aside.

Ted was now behind the controls of his beloved helicopter. The loud whining noise indicated engine ignition. George moved but then paused to glance back towards Ross. 'There's another reason I don't like the idea as well. If we take a doctor with us to all our jobs we'll end up just watching any major interventions like intubation or chest decompression. If we don't keep our own case numbers up we'll lose our skills. It could be dangerous.'

'Good point.' Ross raised his voice over the increasing engine noise. The rotors were starting to turn slowly. 'Bring it up at the next meeting.'

'I will. I'd better go now, Snow.'

Ross gave her a thumbs-up signal. 'Good luck.'

George ducked her head and ran to the waiting helicopter. She slid the door shut behind her and reached for her crash helmet, jamming it over the lump her ponytail presented. She muttered her annoyance and Murray raised his eyebrows. George flicked the small microphone arm into place in front of her mouth and clicked it on.

'I said I'm going to cut my hair. I'm sick of squashing it under this helmet.'

'Don't do that, George.' It was Ted's voice coming through the earphones inside the helmet. 'It's been looking better every day since you started growing it. Much more feminine.'

'Ha!' George scowled. That was the very reason she had never liked her hair with any length to speak of. So why hadn't she had more than a trim for so long?

The helicopter lifted off the pad smoothly and George looked over her shoulder past Ted's knees to where the other base staff were watching their departure. Ross was the closest, his thatch of black hair flattened by the rotor wash. George shook her head. His nickname of 'Snow' was as inappropriate as her own label unless you knew that Ross's surname was 'White'. She could see the lanky frame of Mike 'Stretch' Bingham, and Harry was beside him—laughing as usual. Harry's cheerful demeanour had earned him the nickname of Polly—short for Pollyanna.

Murray was Mozzie and Ted Scott was 'Red' due to his hair colour. You simply weren't one of the team unless you had a nickname and Georgina Collins had been christened five years ago when she'd become the first woman to join the team of helicopter paramedics. She was 'Big George'. One of the boys and proud of it. George was as capable and dedicated as any of them and her hairstyle had always been one of the most closely cropped of the entire team. Had the accident been responsible for that much of a change?

Connected by radio transmission through their helmets, the crew members were able to converse freely despite the noise of the helicopter. George listened as Ted and Murray finalised route plans, notified air traffic control and got an update on weather conditions. Facing backwards, George couldn't watch the unfolding landscape with any comfort so she gave up and closed her eyes. She had seen it all before—many times. The patchwork of the flat Canterbury plains with their bright yellow crops, squares of verdant pasture, the almost black patches of the radiata pine plantations and the blue of small lakes and larger rivers. She was well used to the long New Zealand coastline, the view of the open sea, and wasn't even particularly stirred today by the awe-inspiring beauty of the Southern Alps which they were currently heading towards.

A faint groan escaped George's lips as the helicopter dipped suddenly, buffeted by the strong northwesterly wind.

'Not feeling sick, are you, George?' Ted sounded astonished.

'Of course not,' George responded with slight irritation. 'I'm never sick.'

'You don't sound very happy.'

'I'm happy,' George assured the pilot.

'I'm not,' Murray's voice cut in. 'My name will be mud if I miss Sophie's party.'

'You're not the only one,' Ted told him. 'It's my wedding anniversary today. I've got a dinner reservation at the most expensive joint in town at 8.30 p.m.'

'Put your foot down, then, mate.' George could hear the grin in Murray's tone. 'We've both got a good reason to get this job over and done with.'

George was silent. She didn't have a pressing need to get back home. No celebration to be enjoyed. No ties that an extra hour or even ten could really aggravate. No family at all unless you counted the ill assorted menagerie that shared her life. George might be an entrenched member of the helicopter rescue team but it wasn't just her gender or the length of her hair that now made her stand out as being so different. The others were almost all family men.

It was only George that had had to sacrifice such a huge amount to pursue this career path but she had never regretted the choice. Not really. She was doing exactly what she wanted to do. She *was* happy. She wouldn't even give up any of her different and difficult pets. George suppressed an errant and inexplicable sigh.

'How many years is it, Red?' she asked.

'Twenty-eight,' Ted Scott answered proudly.

'Wow!' George was suitably impressed. 'You must have got married young.'

'I was twenty-five,' Ted responded. 'I met Margaret at an air force ball and it was love at first sight. We got married six weeks later.'

'You're lucky it lasted,' George commented. 'You didn't have much time to get to know each other.'

'Didn't need it,' Ted said complacently. 'We knew we'd both found the right person. Couldn't have been anyone else for either of us.'

George lapsed back into silence. She envied Ted his confidence but she resented the complacency. How could he have known he wouldn't meet anyone else? She had never felt that sure. If she had, maybe she wouldn't have—

Another lurch jerked George's head back. 'Watch out for the potholes!' George's tone was light-hearted as she tried to dismiss the flash of irritation the turbulence gave her. The usual surge of adrenaline hadn't kicked in yet on this mission but it had been a long day. The MVA had been shortly after they'd started their shift at 7 a.m. and it had been a long job. Satisfying, though. The intubation on the overweight truck driver had been a difficult task. George would have had to ask Murray for assistance if that third attempt had also failed.

The babies had been a bit heart-wrenching, tiny scraps of humanity fighting for survival, and the mother had been distraught at there being no room for her to accompany the twins by air. George shook her head. She'd spent too much time already today, thinking about those babies. During the evacuation there had been little for her to do, thanks to the medical escort the babies had had, so George had simply watched, finding herself unable to take her eyes off the two infants. The perfect little hands and feet. The tiny faces with their dark, bewildered eyes. What a sad way to begin life, encased in incubators and attached to monitors and IV lines. She hoped they would both survive to learn the comfort of their mother's arms.

George tried to tune in to the conversation Ted and Murray were now having but they were comparing the ages of their children. It could take a while. Sophie was the oldest of Murray's five children. Ted now had his first grandchild to boast about. It certainly wasn't a topic that George could make a contribution to, although her colleagues often referred to her pets as though they were children. If she had considered them substitute children herself she would have made a better job of selecting them. George smiled wryly to herself. Who else could have collected a diabolically badly behaved donkey, a long-retired, geriatric Clydesdale horse, a grumpy goat and one very calculating cat. None of them had been a conscious choice for a life companion, let alone a substitute child. Various twists of fate had led to their accumulation. Hardly run-of-the-mill pets but, then, Georgina Collins wasn't exactly ordinary either.

Maybe she was tired of being so different. George closed her eyes more firmly this time. With a bit of luck she might even catch a few minutes' sleep before they reached the foothills of the Alps.

'Wakey, wakey!'

George opened her eyes smartly. 'How close are we?'

'That's Minchin Pass down there.' The helicopter was circling. 'We're just trying to pick out the track.'

George craned her neck for a view. They were over a tussock-covered saddle, low enough for the rotor wash to send spectacular wave-like ripples through the long, golden ground cover. She glanced over the surrounding rugged terrain.

'Cloud cover's a bit low.'

'You're not wrong there.' Ted sounded calm but George could sense his tension. 'It's not helping the light either.'

George unclipped her safety belt. 'I'll pack a bum bag,' she announced. 'We won't want to take any extra time winching the trauma pack. What do you reckon, Mozzie? Splint, dressings and IV?'

Murray nodded. 'Take ten of morphine and some Maxolon. Just get a line in and some pain relief. We'll set up IV fluids once we've got him on board.'

'Stretcher or nappy?'

'It's only a tib and fib. Take the nappy.'

George nodded. The nappy was a harness that allowed a patient to be winched up, attached to the crew member. It was uncomfortable for the victim but far more efficient in terms of time. It took very little time to pack the bag and buckle it around her hips. George refastened her seat belt as Murray tapped on his side window.

'There's Locke Hut on the Taramakau.' He pointed out. They followed the river for a brief time. 'That'll be Townsend Creek joining the river, there. Eleven o'clock, five hundred metres.'

'Roger.' The helicopter banked to the right and George caught a glimpse of the small rocky creek threading uphill and frequently obscured by bush.

'I see something,' George exclaimed, seconds later. 'Three o'clock—maybe two hundred metres.'

'Roger.' The helicopter dipped sharply with the change of direction and George tried not to consider the adverse weather conditions. It would be extremely frustrating to have to abandon the rescue mission at this point but the safety of the craft and its crew had to be the first priority. It was up to Ted to make any final decision.

'Target sighted.' Ted had also caught sight of the bright scrap of fabric being waved. As they came closer they could see a figure standing on an outcrop of boulders that created a picturesque waterfall in the creek. He was waving what appeared to be a scarlet T-shirt. The man scrambled down from his vantage point as the helicopter approached and it was then that the figure lying on the ground a little further downhill was spotted. The outcrop of boulders was the clearest spot in a thickly forested area.

'Turning downwind,' Ted informed them.

'Roger. Secure aft.' Murray was leaning forward as he focused on the ground. 'I have the target.' He switched his concentration to the winch control panel. 'Checking winch power,' he announced calmly.

'Turning base leg.' Ted's information came seconds later.

'Roger.' Murray glanced at George who nodded. She automatically checked the security of her harness and seat belt. Ted was turning the helicopter across the wind, getting ready for the final run. It felt rough but the pilot was clearly happy enough with his control of the situation to continue the run and make an attempt to winch her in.

'Final two hundred metres to run.'

'Roger.' There wasn't long to wait for the next well-practised step in the procedure. There was no time to do anything but think and act within the protocol.

'Speed back. Clear door.' Ted's tone was clipped.

George could hear and feel the change in the helicopter as the speed dropped. She watched Murray slide open the side door.

'Door back and locked,' Murray informed Ted. 'Bringing hook inboard.'

George took the large hook in her gloved hands and attached it to her harness. She checked that the pit pin was secure before giving Murray a thumbs-up and unclipping her seat belt.

'One hundred and fifty metres to run.'

'Roger.' Murray still sounded calm. 'Moving George across to door. Clear skids.' He was asking the pilot's permission to put his crewman into a position standing on the helicopter skids. He would also be standing on the skids and leaning out as he controlled the winching and gave vital directional instructions and safety clearances to the pilot. Ted had to make allowances for the extra weight on that side of the helicopter.

'Clear skids,' he affirmed.

Murray faced forward, leaning past George's shoulder as she stood on the skids facing into the helicopter and bracing herself against the icy blast of air current.

'One hundred metres,' Murray reported. 'Eighty…sixty… Clear to boom out.'

'Clear,' Ted responded.

George could feel her weight being taken up completely by the harness. She took a deep breath as she was lowered to a level about three metres below the skids.

'Booming out, boomed out.' Murray told Ted. 'Minus fifty. Minus forty. Clear to winch out.'

'Clear.'

George could not see the target beneath her now. Both she and Ted were now depending on Murray to direct her descent and watch both the main and tail rotor clearances from the trees. The patter from the winch operator was continuous as the helicopter hovered and George was lowered towards the ground. She shut her eyes momentarily. This was always the point when she had to assert real control over her fear. She knew she could do it but it had become a conscious part of the routine for her now. It had been, ever since the accident.

'Good height, well clear,' she heard Murray say. 'How's your distance, George?'

George was watching the ground carefully now. Ted knew how high he was keeping the helicopter and Murray knew how much of the winch cable he had released, but it was up to her to monitor how far her feet were from the

ground once they got this close. 'Minus fifteen,' she told him. 'Ten…nine…eight…'

George's descent slowed considerably as the
distance from the ground went into single figures. Murray was aiming for the most level
patch, just above the outcrop of boulders. The
rocks were wet on that side and George's feet
touched, slipped and then touched again as the
cable gave her a little more slack.

'Weight is coming off,' Murray informed
Ted.

George unhooked herself rapidly. She extended her right arm, with her hand held palm
upwards and gave another thumbs-up to
Murray. The hook was retracted and the helicopter gained height, moving off to hover at a
safer distance. George ignored the aircraft
now. Her attention was focused on the job she
had to do at ground level. A gust of wind left
a chill dampness on her face and the light was
already noticeably less than it had been only
minutes previously. There was no time to lose.

George scrambled over the rocks, moving
downhill towards the target. The uninjured
tramper had started moving towards her but

George only glanced at him as she kept going towards her patient.

'Are you John?' She had to shout over the noise of the departing helicopter. 'Any change in Dougal's condition?'

'Nothing major.' The absence of a Scottish accent surprised George. 'The sooner we get him to a hospital the better, though. He's in a lot of pain.'

'I can deal with that.' George dropped to her knees beside the injured doctor. 'Hi, Dougal. I'm George—one of the helicopter paramedics. How are you feeling?'

'A hell of a lot better now that you're here.' Dougal looked very pale. He peered more closely at the face within the frame of the helmet. 'Hi, George. I wasn't expecting a woman.'

'I'm the only one on the team.' George returned the grin. 'And we've never met properly in Emergency. I guess you just got lucky.' She stripped off her gloves and felt for a pulse at Dougal's wrist. 'Tell me what the main problem is for you right now.'

'The pain in my leg,' Dougal groaned.

'How's your head?' George's hands were in the surgical gloves she had worn beneath the leather ones needed for flight. She felt Dougal's skull carefully, noting the lump on one side and the dried blood in his hair.

'It's a bit sore but hardly noticeable compared to my leg.'

'You were knocked out, yes?'

'Only briefly. I can tell you who the prime minister is if you like.'

George smiled briefly. 'I'm sure you'd let me know if you'd noticed any neurological symptoms. What about your neck?'

'It's fine.'

'Any breathing problems?'

'Hurts a bit but I think it's just bruised ribs. No difficulty, really.'

'Abdominal pain?'

'Bit tender under the ribs on my left side. Nothing serious.'

George nodded. She could do a more thorough secondary survey once they had Dougal safely on board the helicopter. Pain relief was a priority now, so that she could splint the broken leg and get her patient ready to winch.

'Are you allergic to any medications that you know of?'

'No.'

'I'll get an IV line in and give you some morphine for the pain.'

'Cool.' Dougal looked impressed. 'I didn't think you'd be able to manage that so quickly. I thought I'd have to wait until we got out of here.'

'Bit more humane to give you something before we move you.' George only remembered about the laceration to Dougal's forearm when she pulled back the sleeve of his bush shirt and exposed the handkerchief knotted in place. 'How bad is that laceration?'

'Might need a stitch or two. It's stopped bleeding.'

'OK. I'll deal with that later.'

Dougal's nod of agreement turned into an admiring head shake. 'I wasn't expecting a woman,' he told her again. He looked over George's shoulder. 'What do you reckon, Max? George here is a woman.'

Max? But the man's name was John. George's heart stopped for a split second. It *couldn't* be.

It just couldn't.

George turned her head. The man hadn't shaved for several days by the look of him. The woolly Balaclava covered his head but the eyes were dark enough. Now that the helicopter had gone his voice was only too familiar when he spoke again.

'I'm probably more aware of that fact that you are, Dougal.' The voice was calm, almost resigned. 'And I can't say I'm surprised. I was half expecting it might be her.'

'What?' Dougal looked puzzled.

'You said your name was John,' George accused him. It was a stupid thing to say. She knew as well as he did that his name *was* John. John Maxwell. But nobody, least of all his friends, called him anything but Max. And George had been much, much more than a friend. She felt disturbed that she hadn't recognised him instantly despite his heavy stubble and the head covering. 'You'd have to be the last person I was expecting to find on the top of a mountain, Max.'

'Hang on a minute.' Dougal pushed himself into a half-sitting position, dislodging the extra jacket tucked around his shoulders. His face

twisted with pain and George was instantly reminded of why she was here and the pressure
of time. She turned back to Dougal, unzipping
the pouch strapped to her waist.

'Stay still,' she directed. 'Let's get this IV
line in and give you some pain relief. Then
we'll get your leg sorted and get you out of
here.'

'No, wait!' Dougal pulled his hand away
from the approaching tourniquet. 'Do you two
know each other?'

'You could say that.' George captured
Dougal's wrist, pushed the shirtsleeve back
again and clipped the tourniquet in place, tight-
ening it with a rapid flick of her hand. 'Though
''knew'' might be more appropriate. It was
rather a long time ago.'

'Five years,' Max added. 'I told you about
George, Dougal, when I first arrived in
Glasgow and you wanted to know what the
women in New Zealand were like.'

'Yes, but you said...' Dougal paused as he
watched George remove the items she needed
to establish an IV line. His mouth stretched
into a disbelieving smile as his gaze shifted to

George's face. 'No…' he breathed. 'You can't be!'

George caught the astonished gaze. 'Can't be what?' she queried briskly. She ripped open an antiseptic wipe.

Dougal's smile broadened. 'I guess you must be,' he said with amusement.

'Must be what?' George's curiosity was tempered by rising irritation. What *had* Max said to his new friend all those years ago in the wake of their recently broken engagement? Nothing flattering by the look on Dougal's face. She frowned.

'What must I be?' she demanded. 'You'd better get it off your chest so that we can get on with this.'

Dougal shook his head and lay back again. 'Spider Woman,' he murmured with appreciation.

'Excuse me?' George was quite sure she couldn't possibly have heard him correctly, partly due to the warning growl that Max emitted at the same time.

Dougal ignored his friend's warning, slowly nodding with satisfaction as George swabbed the vein on the back of his hand with the wipe.

'Spider Woman,' he repeated clearly. 'Finally—it all makes perfect sense.'

CHAPTER TWO

Spider Woman?

Spider Woman?

'Ouch!' Dougal's arm jerked and the vein George had targeted on the back of his hand lost any contact with the needle.

'Sorry.' George's apology was automatic but terse. 'You should know better than to move like that, Dougal,' she admonished. 'You're a doctor, for goodness' sake. I'll have to do it again now.' Luckily, George had spare supplies in her pouch.

'Sorry, George.' Dougal sounded contrite. He grinned at her disarmingly. 'I'm just more used to being the one on the other end of the needle. I guess I'm a wimp.'

George didn't return the smile. Spider Woman? She rubbed Dougal's forearm with her finger to locate another nice straight length of vein.

'Would you like me to do that for you?' Max sounded as though he was astonished that

anyone could have missed such an easy ve-
nepuncture, even on a moving target.

'No, I wouldn't,' George snapped. She slid
the cannula into place, snapped a connecting
plug onto the end, then tore off pieces of tape
with her teeth to secure the line firmly. She
flicked Max a scathing glance as she snapped
the top from an ampoule of morphine. She
snorted incredulously as she drew the medication into the syringe already containing saline.

'*Spider Woman?*' she enunciated with deliberate scorn.

Max had the grace to look embarrassed.
Dougal had the cheek to chuckle. George was
forced to watch her patient carefully for any
signs of an adverse reaction as she injected
part of the syringe's contents.

'Max never said exactly *what* you did,'
Dougal told her helpfully. 'He implied that you
found your career more appealing than him.'
Dougal wasn't showing any signs of a reaction
to the opiate. 'I always imagined some steely
business-type executive, clutching a briefcase
and cellphone, climbing the corporate web.'

'How's the pain level now?' George inquired stiffly.

'Great!'

'On a scale of one to ten?'

'I'd give it a two.'

'OK.' George withdrew the syringe from the plug and recapped it. 'I've only given you 3 mg. We can top it up if you need it, when I splint your leg.'

'I've already done that,' Max informed her.

'What with—a stick?'

'Two sticks, actually.'

'It's an open fracture, yes?' George refused to show how impressed she was by the straight line of Dougal's lower leg. 'Did you cover the wound with a sterile dressing?'

'A non-stick Telfa pad.' Max sounded less confident this time. 'But the wound is contaminated. I didn't have anything I could flush it with.'

'That can wait,' George decided. The sudden gust of wind that drove a spatter of raindrops audibly onto her helmet was a worry. She glanced up. The cloud cover was moving faster as the front approached. As if in response to her upward glance, her radio crackled into life. She could also see the helicopter closing the distance between them as she pulled her microphone into place and responded to Murray's call.

'It'll only take me a minute to get the nappy on Dougal,' she asserted. 'We're ready to roll.'

'Sorry, George, but we can't risk it.'

George knew better than to protest. Ted wouldn't abandon her unless he absolutely had to.

'I've got the trauma and survival packs on the winch. We're going to try and get them down to the spot you landed.' The contact crackled with static and George tilted her head as she concentrated. 'Can you receive?'

'Roger.' George rose smoothly to her feet and started moving towards the creek bed again. She could see the packs being lowered now, swinging on the end of the winch cable in the wind. Ted was having difficulty keeping the helicopter in position. George crouched as low as she could to avoid being hit by the load. She was angered to notice that Max had followed her and was still standing.

'Get *down*!' she shouted above the roar of the helicopter rotors, motioning fiercely with her arm to emphasise the urgency. 'You idiot,' she added for good measure.

'Weight's off.' Murray's voice sounded clearer for a moment. 'Be quick, George.'

She scuttled towards the delivery, boots slipping uncomfortably on the wet rocks, un-hooked the winch and then held it away from her body and above her head. She extended her other arm and gave the thumbs-up signal. The hook disappeared rapidly upwards. The heli-copter was moving away already.

'Sorry, George.' Murray sounded sincere. 'See you in the morning.'

'Have a great birthday party.' George stared after the departing helicopter for several sec-onds. This was a disaster. Not for her patient. George was quite confident that she had ev-erything she needed to care for Dougal. It was the thought of being stuck on a mountaintop for the night with John Maxwell that was far more of a worry.

'Where the hell are they going?' Max was also staring at the now distant aircraft.

'It's too dangerous to attempt a winching operation.'

'They got those packs down.'

'That's different,' George said impatiently. 'It's not quite as important if they have to get dropped or get tangled in the trees. A person would be too risky.'

'I thought taking risks was part of the job. The attractive part.'

George reached for the straps of the larger pack.

'I'll carry that.'

She ignored the offer. She slipped the pack onto her back and picked up the smaller load. 'We take risks all the time,' she informed Max coolly. 'Calculated risks. But we're not stupid.' She stepped past Max as a flash of sheet lightning illuminated the rapidly darkening skyline. The crack of thunder followed almost immediately and George was surprised by the level of concern on Max's face.

'Don't worry.' It felt satisfying to be able to sound reassuring. 'I'm trained to deal with these sorts of situations.'

Max's black look suggested that George's leadership wasn't welcome. He followed her back to Dougal in a tense silence. Rain was now falling quite steadily and Dougal was holding the extra jacket over his head like an umbrella.

'Where's the taxi gone?' The light-hearted tone didn't match the expression in Dougal's eyes. George crouched close.

'Sorry, Dougal. It was too dangerous to get you out with the chopper. We'll have to dig in for the night. If the weather clears they'll be back at first light, otherwise they'll send a ground crew in to meet us.'

'My timing was lousy, wasn't it?' Dougal tried to smile.

'Don't worry. I've got all sorts of goodies in these packs.' George eased the trauma pack from her back and patted it as she set it down. 'I promise I'll keep you comfortable.' She took a deep breath. 'The first priority is to establish some decent shelter. Are you guys carrying a tent?'

'No. We've been using the huts.'

'Do you have sleeping bags? Cooking equipment?'

'Of course,' Max snapped. 'We're not stupid.'

'Good.' George rose to her feet. 'I've got a canvas ground sheet in my survival pack.

We'll build a windbreak with brushwood and then attach the sheet as a roof.' She scanned the hillside. 'Let's get further in under the trees. We're too exposed to the wind right here and the water level in that creek is going to rise with this rain.'

'Have you ever spent a night on a mountainside before?' Max queried.

'Yes, I have,' George responded promptly. 'I've had plenty of survival training.'

'Training exercises.' Max sounded dubious. 'Have you ever spent a night in the open in weather like this? In a situation that involves a real patient?'

George shook her head with exasperation. 'Let's discuss this later, shall we?' She extracted the rolled-up canvas sheet from her survival pack. 'Hold this over Dougal and yourself and keep dry while I get the windbreak set up. I don't want to have to deal with any cases of hypothermia and you're not even wearing a jacket.' She moved away before Max had a chance to protest at his enforced role as a spectator. She removed her crash helmet, replacing it with a snug woollen hat from her pack. Then she lost no more time in starting her task.

There were plenty of larger broken branches available. She chose a fallen tree trunk as a good base and began to pile building materials beside it.

What would Max say if he knew that the only time she had been caught in the open in a situation involving a patient she had *been* the patient? The training exercise had gone horribly wrong. With the winch cable fouled in the treetops, the only way to prevent the craft crashing had been to cut the cable. The tree had broken George's fall to some extent but it had not prevented the spinal fracture which had left her immobilised and terrified for the length of time it had taken to get a second helicopter to the scene and a rescue team winched in to help her.

George knew exactly what Max would say. He would be delighted to remind her just how often he had protested that the career she had dreamed about was far too dangerous for anyone but particularly for a woman. That what she should be doing was giving up her ambitions and settling for the safe and fulfilling role of being a wife and mother. Well, George wasn't going to give him the satisfaction of being able to say, 'I told you so.'

Even the pride with which she had walked out of the spinal injuries unit eight weeks after the accident wouldn't be worth sharing. Or the personal achievement of overcoming any residual physical and psychological barriers to a return to full employment within six months of the injury. The simple 'I told you so' would negate that pride. If she hadn't been stupid enough to insist on such a dangerous career in the first place, she would never have had to face the challenge of dealing with the consequences.

George snapped small, leafy branches from the undergrowth, piling a good layer over the framework of branches wedged behind and over the log. It was a dense enough wall to break the icy wind quite satisfactorily. When the canvas sheet was anchored to the top and ground, the tent-shaped shelter would provide sufficient, if somewhat cosy, accommodation for three people. The ground beneath the layer of leaf mulch was surprisingly dry and George's final preparation was to open out

Dougal's sleeping bag in the centre of the floor space.

With an arm around both Max's and George's shoulders, and the benefit of more pain relief, Dougal was able to hop the short distance to the shelter. He lay down again with a groan.

'We'll get any wet clothing off you first,' George decided. 'Then I want to give you a thorough check-up, treat that fracture and get you as warm and comfortable as possible.'

'Sounds good to me,' Dougal agreed.

George's examination of her patient was thorough. Conscious of the scrutiny she was under from a man whom she knew had been working as an emergency department consultant in Glasgow for the last five years, George was meticulous in conducting a secondary survey. She checked Dougal out from head to toe, looking carefully for any indication of repercussions from the head injury and the bruised area over his ribs. She cleaned up and redressed the laceration on his arm before finally turning her attention again to the fractured leg. She unwrapped the blood stained crêpe bandage covering Dougal's shin carefully.

'You've lost a bit of blood here,' she commented. 'And that bruising over your ribs is severe enough to push the volume up a bit. I'm going to set up some fluid replacement as soon as we've finished this. I'll use one litre of saline to flush out the worst of the debris from this fracture, though.' George glanced at Dougal. 'It's not going to be very pleasant. Do you want some more morphine?'

Dougal smiled stoically but then nodded. 'I wouldn't mind a bit of metaclopromide as well, if you've got some.'

'Sure. Are you feeling sick?'

'A bit.'

Max had listened to the exchange silently. He caught George's eye and jerked his head. It was a subtle movement but quite enough to indicate that he wanted to talk to her privately.

'I'll just get that billy I saw in your pack,' she told Dougal. 'That way we can catch the run-off from the flushing and won't get your sleeping bag wet.' She ducked through the opening between the fly sheet and the brushwood wall.

'I'll see what the chances are like for getting a fire going,' Max said casually as he followed

George. 'Don't know about you but I could sure use a hot cup of tea.'

It was quite dark outside the shelter now. The wind was blowing hard and the rain was relentless. Max had piled more brushwood over the extra packs there was no room for inside. They both moved towards the make-shift storage area.

'You'll never get a fire going in this,' George observed.

'Don't need to,' Max responded. 'I've got a Primus we can use inside. I just wanted to talk to you.' He looked serious. 'How much fluid replacement have you got?'

'Two units of saline and one of Haemaccel.'

'And you're going to use one to irrigate the fracture?'

'Have you got a better suggestion?' George frowned. 'There's gravel and bark and good-ness knows what other material stuck in that wound. The more we can get out the more we can reduce the possibility of infection.'

'It's quite possible he's got internal injuries that aren't obvious yet. Like a lacerated spleen.'

George had already given that possibility considerable thought during her examination of Dougal's bruised ribs. 'His vital signs are fine. If he was losing blood at a significant rate he'd be showing some signs of shock by now. His pulse and respiration rates are normal. His blood pressure is good. The fracture site has stopped bleeding.' George met Max's gaze directly. 'He does have some abdominal tenderness over his spleen so I suppose there could be a slow bleed. What say we swab out what we can from the fracture site, use half a unit of saline to flush and keep a slow IV drip going?' And hope for the best, George added silently.

'We can get some fluids in orally as well. It's not as though he's heading for surgery anytime soon,' Max added. 'I'll get that tea made, as soon as we've cleaned up the fracture.'

George felt pleased that Max wasn't going to argue about her treatment plan. She also liked the implication that he planned to assist her. Collecting the extra items they needed, they returned to the shelter.

'It was a good splinting job,' George congratulated Max.

'I expect you intend to replace it.' His tone was a challenge.

George shook her head. 'The sticks are far enough away from the wound not to contaminate it. I'll put a cardboard backing on, a sterile dressing on top and we can leave the rest as it is and rebandage it. The limb baselines aren't bad at all. I don't want to challenge them by possibly altering the alignment.'

Drops of water rolled off the Balaclava and down his face as Max tilted his head in acknowledgement. He peeled off the head covering and hung it on a protruding branch end at the side of the shelter. George couldn't help staring for a moment. She had almost forgotten that unique streak of naturally white hair above Max's left temple. In the midst of thick black waves, it had always stood out as one of the most distinctive aspects of Max's appearance. In recent years, however, when she remembered his face, it had been the dark, virtually black eyes she thought of first. The incongruously gentle gaze that came from an otherwise rugged face. Very rugged at the moment with the heavy stubble shadowing the lower half.

'Have you got a pair of gloves my size?'

George's gaze flicked hurriedly downwards. She had forgotten the size of Max's hands as well. Large, square, masculine hands with a smattering of hair as dark as his head. They looked strong enough to demolish a building but she knew, only too well, the kind of gentleness they, too, were capable of. The reminder caused only a momentary disturbance, a split second of distraction, but it was enough to create a wash of warmth that threatened to colour George's cheeks to a noticeable degree even in the dim light the camp lantern was providing within the shelter.

'I've only got mediums. They'll be a bit of a squeeze.'

'Doubt if I'll even get them on. How 'bout I just do the non-sterile bits?'

It worked well. Max held the torch to illuminate the wound as George used wet gauze swabs and sterile tweezers to pick out the larger pieces of debris. Max supported Dougal's leg as George used a giving set attached to the bag of saline as a tiny hose to flush the smaller particles out, keeping the billy in place to catch the run-off. Finally, they were done. With his leg dressed, rebandaged and elevated, a dry woollen bush shirt on and his sleeping bag zipped up warmly, Dougal looked very pale but much happier.

George attached a new giving set to the unit of saline, connected it to the IV line in Dougal's forearm, hung the bag from a convenient branch end and adjusted the flow to a slow, steady drip. Max brought in enough dry contents of their own packs to cushion the log as a back rest, then he cleaned out the billy and emptied a bottle of drinking water into it.

The small Primus was efficient and Max dropped the teabags into the boiling water only minutes later. The mug of tea, heavily laced with sweetened, condensed milk from the tube Max offered, was the most delicious-smelling drink George had ever encountered in her entire life.

'Thanks, Max.' She paused with the mug only halfway to her lips, puzzled by the stare she was receiving. 'What's the problem?'

'First time you've smiled at me,' Max responded. He was still staring.

'There hasn't been much to smile about.' George sipped the drink. 'This, however, is a winner.'

Max reached for his own mug. 'I might even cook you some dinner, if you're lucky.'

'Meat loaf?' The scornful suggestion popped out from nowhere. 'I don't think I'm that hungry.'

'I didn't see any dehydrated meat loaf in the trekking supplies shop.' Dougal was drinking his own tea with obvious enjoyment. 'Sounds nice.'

'She's not talking about camping supplies,' Max snorted. 'George never did think much of my cooking.'

'Only the meat loaf.'

'What else did I cook?'

George's lips twisted into a wry smile. 'That is a valid question. Not much, I guess.'

'Exactly.' Max glanced at Dougal. 'Fortunately, I've learned a thing or two since then. Flatting with Dougal here, I was forced to learn to cook in order to survive.'

'I can cook,' Dougal protested. 'I'm a great cook!'

'Yeah.' Max was grinning at his friend. 'But there's only so much black pudding one man can stand. We won't even mention the haggis.'

'No, don't!' George was caught by the obvious bond of friendship and humour between the two men. 'Please, don't mention the haggis.'

Max's grin faded instantly and George knew he wasn't about to forgive her taunt about the meat loaf. Dougal seemed unaware of the undercurrent of tension.

'I still can't believe you're Spider Woman, George,' Dougal said cheerfully. 'You do realise you broke Max's heart, don't you?'

'Yeah, right,' George muttered. She buried her nose behind the wide rim of the tin mug.

'He's never looked at another woman. Not seriously.'

George said nothing. Was that true? Had Max been unable, like herself, to find anyone who could fill that particular void?

The dismissive snort from Max put paid to that notion. 'What about Rowena?' he challenged Dougal. 'I went out with her for three years.'

'Mmm.' Dougal was looking drowsy which was hardly surprising given the amount of morphine he had circulating. 'Great knitter, Rowena.'

'Sounds perfect for you, Max.' Why did these spiteful comments keep pushing themselves past George's lips? 'Nice little wife who would stay safely at home, knitting bootees.'

Dougal snorted with laughter. 'I doubt Rowena would even know what a bootee was for. No, jerseys were her specialty. Like that one Max is wearing.'

George glared at the beautifully knitted, fawn Aran jersey covering Max's broad shoulders. She hated the garment. Too fussy by half.

'And as for staying home...' Any perception of how unwelcome the line of conversation might be was clearly dulled by the drug-induced euphoria Dougal was enjoying. 'Rowena was very English. Grew up on a country estate. Outdoorsy. She hiked up every hill Scotland had to offer. Horsy type, you know?'

'I know,' George agreed readily. 'Big teeth.'

'God, no. She was gorgeous!' There was no stopping Dougal Donaldson. 'Wild red hair and green eyes. Half the hiking club were in love with Rowena but it was our Max she set her sights on.' Dougal became aware of his friend's lack of participation in the conversation. 'You should have brought her on holiday with you, Max. She'd love New Zealand.'

'I haven't seen Rowena for a while.' Max was giving nothing away by his tone. 'She took leave of absence from the hospital to go home and care for her father when he had a stroke.'

'So Rowena's a nurse, then?' George queried politely.

'No, she's a surgeon. Neurology department.'

Of course. A brain surgeon. Not only gorgeous, she was brilliant. Rowena whatever-her-last-name-was could stride over mountains, probably knitting complicated jerseys as she went. George took a very deep breath. Why on earth should she be consumed by such an unreasonable—and unpleasant—feeling of jealousy? What had she expected Max to do? Go off and live like a monk for the rest of his life because things hadn't worked out with her? Yes. George had to admit that the scenario did have a certain appeal. She flashed

Max a 'men are all the same' glance and was annoyed to find herself under a steady and calm scrutiny.

'I think I'll take your vital signs again, Dougal.' George pushed her mug away and opened her trauma pack to extract the blood-pressure cuff. 'It's at least an hour since I last checked.'

George was using a hand-held radio transmitter to keep in touch with the search and rescue base in Arthur's Pass, turning it off between transmissions to save battery power. She established contact again, after checking Dougal, relieved to report no significant deterioration in her patient's condition. She was also relieved to hear that Murray and Ted had made it back to town safely and that a new mission was planned for first light. According to the Met. office, the southerly blast should be sharp but short and could clear any time in the next few hours. Judging by the sound of the rain pelting onto the canvas fly sheet, the clearance wasn't imminent, however.

Dougal slept for a while and George busied herself writing a report on the incident by the light of a torch. She detailed Dougal's injuries and treatment so far. Then George checked her drug supplies, wondering how much more morphine Dougal might require before tidying the whole pack, setting aside supplies that might be needed during the night. Max was as quiet as she was and just as busy, preparing a meal over the Primus stove. He added boiling water to a dehydrated food mix sachet, setting it aside to soak as he cooked pasta in the remaining boiling water. Dougal woke up as Max passed George a very welcome plate of hot food.

'I hope spaghetti Bolognese is acceptable.'

'Looks great.' George knew she deserved the slightly sarcastic tone. 'Thanks.' She caught Max's eye but couldn't hold the contact for more than the time it took to give a brief, polite smile. Her gaze slid towards Dougal. 'How are you feeling, Dougal?'

'Leg's a bit sore again,' Dougal admitted.

'How's the tummy pain?'

Dougal cautiously felt the area. 'About the same. I've got a splitting headache, though.'

George put her plate down and picked up her penlight torch. She crawled closer to Dougal. 'Bright light again,' she warned. 'I want to check your pupils.' She clicked the torch off seconds later and held a single finger in front of her nose.

'Follow my finger with your eyes,' she instructed. 'Don't move your head.' George moved her finger from side to side and up and down. Dougal's tracking movements appeared normal. His pupils were equal and reactive. He had no discoloration of the skin around his eyes or behind his ears and no discharge of fluid from his ears or nose. The lump on his head had reduced in size but was still very tender.

'You could have a skull fracture,' George told him, 'but I can't see any signs of rising intracranial pressure that might suggest a subdural or epidural haematoma.' She smiled, relaxing again. 'With a bump that was hard enough to knock you out, you're bound to have a concussion. You'll probably have a headache for a few days.' George checked her watch. 'It's nearly four hours since the last dose of morphine. I could top that up if you like.'

'Thanks.' Dougal settled back against the padded log.

'Let me do that.' Max put down his half-eaten meal. 'Your dinner's going to be stone cold at this rate.'

'OK.' George accepted the offer gratefully, stifling a yawn. It was now after midnight and it had been a long day. She flicked her torch on to confirm the drug and expiry date of the ampoules Max took from her kit and then left him to it, climbing into her sleeping bag before picking up her plate.

Even lukewarm, the meal was wonderful and George ate ravenously. By the time Max had checked that the IV was still running freely, had administered the drugs and run through another vital sign check on his friend, George was scraping the last of the pasta from her plate.

'I like to see a woman enjoying her food,' Dougal said.

'It was good.' George grinned. 'I'm impressed. Thanks, Max.'

'You were probably hungry enough to appreciate even meat loaf.' Max shrugged off the compliment. 'But you're welcome, anyway.'

'I wish I was hungry,' Dougal said plaintively. 'But I doubt that even a slice of haggis could tempt me right now.'

'How 'bout another cup of tea?' George suggested. 'You'll have a session in Theatre coming up to fix that fracture but it won't be before mid-morning at the earliest. As long as we keep you nil by mouth from about 4 a.m. you'll be OK.'

'Yes, please.' Dougal nodded and then winced. He closed his eyes. 'Throw a dram or two of whisky in it as well and I'll sleep like a baby.'

'I'll put the billy outside and collect some rain water,' Max decided. He grimaced as he glanced beyond the fly sheet. 'It shouldn't take long.'

The mention of sleep had made George yawn again. Max turned his head at the sound. 'You realise that one of us will have to stay awake all night to keep an eye on Dougal?'

'Of course.'

'You look like you're having trouble keeping your eyes open already.'

'I'll manage.' George was defensive. 'I did start my shift nearly eighteen hours ago, you know.'

'I'm not criticising you.' Max sounded weary himself. 'I was going to offer to do the watching. You can go to sleep any time you like.'

'Thanks,' George muttered ungraciously. She had no intention of sleeping on the job. Neither was she going to let Max know she had a backache that sitting on hard ground wasn't helping in the slightest. A headache that might be able to compete with Dougal's was also beginning. But George was doing the job she had sacrificed her relationship with this man to achieve. Demonstrating any lack of ability or satisfaction in meeting the challenge it currently presented was definitely not an option.

The billy filled and was boiled. Max made the tea again. Dougal sipped with noisy pleasure.

'This is almost fun,' he announced.

George debated finding an aspirin tablet in her kit and decided she would rather put up with the discomfort than have to explain why she was taking medication. Casually rubbing her temple, it made George wonder whether the tight ponytail might be contributing to the pain. She took off her woollen hat and pulled the band clear, shaking her head before raking her fingers through the straight, black, shoulder-length tresses.

Max's eyebrows shot up. 'You've grown your hair,' he said disapprovingly.

George allowed the comment to pass with only a shrug. She understood the tone. Max had often encouraged her to grow her hair into a more feminine style. She had always stated that she preferred it short. And she had.

Dougal misinterpreted the disapproval. 'I think it looks great,' he told George. 'Especially loose like that.' His brow creased thoughtfully as he kept his gaze on her. 'What kind of name is George for a woman? Don't you have a real name—like Georgia or Georgette or something?'

'Georgina.' George uttered the name with distaste. 'But the only people who get away with using it are my family.'

'And that's only because she can't beat them into submission.' Max was grinning at Dougal. 'I tell you, mate, you wouldn't want to have been one of George's schoolmates if you dared use her real name in the playground.'

'Really?' Dougal's tone was admiring. 'Feisty wee thing, were you?'

'I was a tomboy,' George admitted, 'but I forced into it by circumstances beyond my control.'

'Do tell.' Dougal sounded fascinated now. Distraction from his present condition was clearly welcome so George was quite happy to oblige. She curled up in her sleeping bag, trying to make herself more comfortable in her position beside Dougal. Her head was already feeling better, having had the tension on her scalp released.

'My mother had three sons. Along with my father they made a kind of men's club that my mother was only too happy to support. I came along unexpectedly about eight years after the youngest son and suddenly my mother had just what she had always wanted—a little girl to dress up and keep pretty.'

'A doll,' Dougal enlarged helpfully. He was listening avidly. Max had eased his long frame into his own sleeping bag. He rolled up an extra bush shirt to put under his head and lay down on the other side of Dougal. The warmth that their close proximity generated helped dispel the worry that they wouldn't be able to deal with the unpleasant environmental conditions. The dim light from the lantern made a contribution that gave the shelter an almost cosy atmosphere. Max was staring up at the join between the brushwood wall and the fly sheet, apparently uninterested in George's story. He had heard most of it before, anyway.

'She must have had two hundred ribbons to choose from when she decorated the ends of my plaits,' George informed Dougal solemnly. 'And a whole cake tin crammed with clips. Flowers, butterflies, plastic bows—you name it, she had spares.'

'Lots of pink ones?' Dougal encouraged.

'Absolutely.' George grinned. 'When I was about seven I got hold of her dressmaking shears, hid inside the macrocarpa hedge and cut my hair off as short as I could. Too short to hold the smallest clip. Mum cried for a week but I was happy. I wanted to look like the boys.'

'Why?' Dougal sounded genuinely puzzled.

George sighed. Dougal was going to be just like everybody else who couldn't really understand. Just like her family. Just like Max.

'I was never allowed to do things I really wanted to do. It was seen as ''boy's stuff''. Things like woodwork, or rugby or playing the drums. The catchphrase in our house always seemed to be, ''Girls aren't supposed to do things like that.'' Even my brothers wanted a pretty little sister they could show off. My mother got angry about it as I got older. She'd say, ''Girls aren't supposed to even *want* to do things like that. Why do you want to be a boy?''.'

'What did you say?' Dougal queried. Max stopped watching the drips forming on the ceiling of the shelter and turned towards George, his expression neutral.

'I always said the same thing,' George responded quietly. 'I said I didn't want to be a *boy*. I just wanted to be *me*.'

'Fair enough.' Dougal nodded. Max was frowning as though concentrating. George was suddenly disconcerted by the attention she was receiving.

'Anyway,' she said lightly, 'life was a bit of a battleground, I suppose. I lost over the ballet and piano lessons. I won with my hairstyle and the horseriding lessons. My mother always refused to watch me compete, though. She thought it was far too dangerous.'

'George was an ace rider,' Max put in unexpectedly. He hadn't spoken for a long time and his voice sounded gruff. 'Three-day eventing, hunting—show jumping. She could handle any horse, any event. And win.'

George grunted modestly. The praise was surprising and a little poignant.

'Do you still ride?' Max asked quietly.

George simply shook her head. Riding had been one activity she had given up completely after her accident. All she could cope with now was a very slow walk on the back of her gentle old Clydesdale.

'We rented a place out of the city when we were living together,' Max told Dougal. 'A place that had room for George to keep her horse. Amazing old house—a real mansion. It had about twenty rooms and had had a mad old lady living in it since the days her family had farmed the area. It was the original homestead but it had been let go badly for about fifty years. We rented it for virtually nothing after the old lady got taken off to a rest home.'

Max flicked a glance towards George. 'Where are you living these days?'

'I bought a house.' George's response was deliberately noncommittal. She wasn't going to tell him that six months after he'd left, the old lady had died. The Australian branch of the family had been the only relatives left and they had been at a complete loss as to how to offload such a run-down property so far from the city when there was a slump in the property market. George had picked it up for a song. A lot of her time off in the last five years had been spent making renovations to the interior of the old stone house. Max had loved the property as much as she had. If he knew who the new owner was he would be bound to request a visit, and George didn't want to have to handle that.

Dougal yawned and George wondered if she should encourage him to sleep. The conversation was serving a useful purpose, however. It was keeping her awake and it was much easier to monitor Dougal's condition this way. Any altered mental status due to his head injury or developing shock from internal bleeding would be easily and quickly apparent by his responses.

'My career was a compromise as well,' George told him. 'I wanted to be a doctor but two of my brothers had already achieved that. The other one was a lawyer. I was steered away from science subjects at high school so I retaliated by doing a science degree at university. Then I became a secondary school science teacher.'

'So how did you end up being a paramedic?'

George grinned mischievously. 'I never told Mum but when I wasn't teaching science I was coaching a rugby team. The losers who couldn't make any of the official school teams. They were a neat bunch—really motivated to improve. They tried a bit too hard at times and one day there was an accident, a nasty scrum collapse that left one lad with a spinal injury. I helped the ambulance crew that turned up and rode with them to the hospital. Gave up teaching and joined the ambulance service three weeks later.'

'How old were you then?'

'Twenty-three.'

'And how old are you now?' Dougal continued.

'Thirty-five.'

'And still riding into danger to rescue people.' Max's tone was resigned.

'Can't think of anything else I'd rather be doing.'

'That'd be right.' Now Max sounded bitter. 'Normal life was never exciting enough.'

Normal life with him. Being a normal wife and mother. It was time to change the subject. 'You haven't been in New Zealand very long, have you, Dougal?' George observed. 'How do you like it?'

'Love it,' Dougal responded promptly. 'I have no intention of going back to Scotland.'

'What?' Max was clearly dismayed. 'You can't be serious.'

'I am,' Dougal confirmed.

'What are you planning to do? Apply for residence?'

'Or marry a Kiwi.' Dougal grinned at George. 'In fact, that idea is becoming more attractive by the minute. George, you're the perfect woman.'

'Only because you're full of morphine.' George couldn't help returning the smile.

'No, I mean it,' Dougal insisted. 'You're gorgeous. And brave. And clever...and single, aren't you?'

George laughed to cover her embarrassment. 'Hardly!'

Dougal sighed theatrically. 'Only to be expected, of course. I'd have been surprised if you'd said anything else.' He turned to Max. 'I don't suppose you're surprised either.'

'About what?' Max snapped.

'About George not being single.'

George's jaw dropped. 'I never said I wasn't single.'

'Yes, you did!' Dougal's eyebrows rose. 'I asked—specifically—and you said, "Hardly."'

George's breath was expelled in a dismissive huff. 'I was referring to being the superlative creature your other adjectives described.'

'So you *are* single?' Dougal persisted hopefully.

George hesitated. Dougal was a nice man but she wasn't interested in starting a relationship. Max was staring at her with an odd expression. Did she want to admit that she had failed in that area of her life more than he had? Maybe Max hadn't got married but a three-year relationship with the renowned Rowena had to be significant.

'I suppose so,' George said reluctantly. She wriggled out of her sleeping bag. 'I need a quick trip outside,' she excused herself. 'Nature's calling.'

The heavy rain had finally stopped but, judging by the drizzle, the area was still in the midst of thick cloud. It still sounded very wet thanks to the tumble of water over the nearby boulders of the creek bed and the increased roar of the small waterfall. George sent a silent plea into the night for the weather to clear. The sooner she could get her patient into hospital and herself away from Max, the better. She couldn't even get away from Max for a few seconds now. He had followed her out of the shelter.

'I'd prefer to do this by myself, thanks.'

Max ignored the acerbic comment. 'What do you mean, you *suppose* you're single? Don't you know?'

'Of course I do. And it's none of your business.'

'Maybe you should tell me anyway.' Max took a step closer.

'Why should I?'

'Dougal's a very good friend of mine. He's clearly taken a fancy to you.' Max shrugged as though the attraction was inexplicable in his opinion. 'If he needs warning off then I should tell him.'

'I can warn my own men off, thank you,' George said crisply. Not that she was managing that feat too well right now. She took a step back but Max filled the gap instantly.

'You're not doing a very good job of it.'

Damn it. Had Max become a mind-reader in his spare time? 'What's that supposed to mean?' George could feel the heat coming from Max's body thanks to the sub-zero chill surrounding them. They shouldn't be standing around outside but Max wasn't about to let her escape.

'You *suppose* you're single,' he bit out. 'Dougal probably thinks you're waiting around to be rescued from a situation that you're finding is less than what you wanted.'

George was stunned into silence. Did she have a situation that was less than she wanted? Like her life? Yes. But did she want to be rescued? Of course. But not by Dougal Donaldson. She tried to sound nonchalant.

'What I meant was that I'm not in a relationship but that I'm also not interested. I have more important things in my life right now.'

'Like your career, I suppose.' Max's tone rankled.

'That's right.' It *was* true. She had to make some decision about her career. George had reached another turning point in her life. It had been building ever since the accident and now George knew she couldn't avoid the issue any longer.

'So.' Max sounded disgusted. 'Nothing much has changed, then, has it?'

George looked at Max. She could see beneath the exhaustion, the stubble and the anger. She could see the man she had once fallen so much in love with. She could feel the heat from his body like a solid force now and knew that it wouldn't take much of a spark to ignite the flames of the same physical desire that had been so overwhelming all those years ago.

'No,' she agreed quietly. 'Nothing's changed.'

CHAPTER THREE

NOTHING had changed.

And yet everything had changed.

The helicopter banked sharply, simultaneously dropping altitude. George's very empty stomach lurched in protest before settling into an unpleasant queasiness. Fatigue and lack of food were a combination that George knew better than to think acceptable in her line of work. Maybe she couldn't have forced her body to sleep but she knew she could have done a lot better than the uninterested snacking she had allowed herself to get away with.

The chopper dipped and turned again before slowing abruptly to a hover. George raised her eyebrows at Mike Bingham who merely shrugged tolerantly in response. Jack 'the Ripper' Burgess, who was piloting the helicopter liked to fly with a flourish. Perhaps the perfect weather that the November day had provided and the easy landing target of a local football field hadn't presented enough of a challenge for the enthusiastic young pilot. George would have vastly preferred being crewed with her usual team of Ted and Mozzie. She wasn't into excitement for its own sake. This job was risky enough without trying to spice it up.

The skids touched ground, bounced a little and then settled. The rotors gradually slowed but wouldn't be stopping. The patient they had been called in to retrieve was a middle-aged man having what appeared to be a major heart attack. He needed to get into the care of the cardiologists at Christchurch hospital as soon as possible.

The local ambulance was a modified four-wheel-drive vehicle operated in conjunction with the rural fire service. The patient had been attended by a GP in the small district hospital of Akaroa on the Banks Peninsula and had already received treatment of aspirin, morphine for the severe central chest pain and metaclopromide to counteract the tendency of the opiate to cause nausea. He'd had an ECG trace taken and his vital signs recorded and was now on high-flow oxygen. There was nothing more that could be done here and it was now over two hours since the man's pain had started.

By road it would have taken an hour and a half to get to Christchurch hospital and after assessment there he would have been outside the four-hour window during which a rescue angioplasty procedure could be done to clear the blocked coronary artery causing the infarct. By helicopter, the team would have him in the emergency department within thirty minutes but there was still no time to waste.

George was first to climb out of the helicopter. She ran at a crouch to clear the rotors. 'Hi, Jerry.' George knew the fire officer standing beside the Jeep.

'G'day, George. Nice day for it.'

'You bet!' George was moving towards the back of the Jeep. 'James Warren—is that the name of our patient?'

'Jim,' Jerry corrected. 'He owns the fish-and-chip shop down by the wharf. Best fish and chips in town,' he added with a grin.

'Hi, Jim. I'm George.' She was pleased to see her patient smiling. George nodded at Andrew, the other fire officer who had transported Jim to the football field. 'Have these boys been looking after you?'

'The only thing they're worried about is where they're going to get their dinner on Friday night.' Jim Warren's voice was a little muffled, both by his oxygen mask and his broad smile.

'That's right, mate.' Jerry was leaning on the end of the stretcher. He winked at George. 'Make sure they get him fixed up nice and fast.'

'How's the pain at the moment, Jim?' George had her hand on her patient's wrist. She was checking out the paperwork at the same time. The twelve-lead ECG showed acute changes in leads II, III and AVF. Judging by the size of the ST elevation, Jim was having a large inferior MI. Baseline recordings of heart and respiration rate, blood pressure, skin colour, pain score and GCS had all been updated within the last five minutes, which was excellent. They wouldn't have to waste any more time.

'A lot better than it was, that's for sure.'

'Can you give it a score out of ten?'

Jim was now used to grading his pain on a scale of zero to ten. Initially a ten, the morphine administered by the GP had brought the rating down to three. Jim decided it hadn't changed since then.

'That's good.' George was surveying her patient. He looked pale but wasn't sweating and didn't look distressed. His respiration rate was normal. 'Have you been in a helicopter before, Jim?'

Jim shook his head and George watched his face closely. 'How do you feel about that?'

George's query seemed a lot more casual that it actually was. Transporting a patient with an acute myocardial infarction required attention to several areas. The blood and oxygen flow to the heart tissues was already compromised and it was George's and Mike's job to control factors that could make the situation worse. Anxiety about flying was one such factor and if the patient was very nervous then sedation would be advisable.

'Can't be any worse than driving with this lot.' Jim waved a hand towards Jerry and Andrew who professed indignation at the insult. George grinned. Anxiety didn't appear to be a problem. She checked the flow of the IV line Jim had in place and then closed it off temporarily as they moved Jim onto the stretcher Mike now had ready, loading their patient efficiently onto the helicopter. George then opened the IV flow to keep the line patent and attached the oxygen-mask tubing to the main cylinder. Mike applied electrodes and got the ECG monitoring in place.

'I'll just get a quick BP,' George decided. 'And then we'll be ready to roll.'

Engine noise was already increasing. ' All set?' Jack queried.

'Almost.'

'Keep it low?' Jack sounded eager.

'Not too low,' George responded calmly. 'Under two thousand feet should be fine.' She turned the oxygen flow up to maximum. It was always important for a patient with reduced blood supply to the heart muscle to be on a high concentration of oxygen. It was another area that required particular attention during air transport, especially at higher altitudes. A height limit of two thousand feet was no problem for the helicopter over flat country but there were some high hills to get over first and

George was aware of another flash of regret that it wasn't Ted piloting them today. This was just the sort of job that Jack Burgess revelled in.

Sure enough, Jack hugged the hills, twisting along valley floors with a panache that made George set her features into uncharacteristically grim lines. She tried to concentrate on the monitoring of their patient. Mike was watching the ECG with some concern due to the extra beats that were disrupting the previously stable rhythm. Jim was trying to tell George something. She leaned closer and lifted the mask for a second.

'How long?' Jim queried.

'For the trip? No more than twenty minutes to go.' George had to shout over the engine noise. 'How are you feeling?'

'Not bad.'

George returned Jim's smile and replaced the mask. She wished she could say the same. Fatigue, lack of food and now the disturbance of Jack's flying style were adding up to a combination that George could well have done without. She shouldn't have been on today at all but, having been left on the side of a mountain for the night, George had been forced to swap a shift with Ross so she could catch up on sleep the following day.

And sleep she had, at least for a while. Sheer exhaustion had ensured that after the mission had finally been completed yesterday morning. Thank God the weather had cleared enough for the mission to be resumed at first light. Both Dougal and Max had been winched clear of the site in textbook fashion. A quick trip to Christchurch and then transfer from the helipad on the hospital roof to the emergency department by hospital staff. Ted had flown George straight back to base. He had offered to fly her all the way home but George hadn't wanted to be stranded so far out of town without her own transport.

'I'll be fine,' she assured Ted. 'I'll drive very carefully and go straight to bed when I get home.'

And she did. George dropped instantly into a dreamless slumber that lasted several hours. With the edge taken off her exhaustion, however, she woke late afternoon to a mental state that alternated between some very disturbing emotions. A whole minefield of long ignored issues suddenly became unavoidable. Every step of her thoughts seemed to set off a charge that made further rest impossible and any appetite unimaginable.

It was the unexpected reappearance of John Maxwell in her life that was responsible and the long, lonely evening and night provided far too many hours to analyse why the effect was so explosive. George's relationship with Max had not been enough for her. She had given it up to follow her career. Now her career wasn't enough for her. Was George doomed to never find satisfaction in her life?

Perhaps the fault lay in her own attitude. Perhaps she now deserved the inevitable and agonised picking over what she had lost when her relationship with Max had ended. What her career offered in terms of a substitute. What it *would* offer in five or ten years' time when she was past coping with the physical demands of her job. The time frame could well be a lot less than that. The backache George had been left with after rescuing Dougal had underlined the emotional aftermath of the mission. It was bad enough to motivate her into arranging a medical check-up for the following week.

All in all, George doubted that she had ever felt quite so miserable. Even after her break-up with Max five years ago. Even after the accident when it had been debatable whether she would walk again let alone go back to the job she loved. On those occasions she'd had a new goal to strive for—an end that had made the suffering worthwhile. What goal did she have now? George was thirty-five years old. She was exactly where she had always wanted to be. And it wasn't enough. Not nearly enough.

The short time that George's introspection took was enough for several things to change on their current mission. Jack had cleared the hills and was now flying level over flat farming land, making a beeline for the hospital helipad. Mike had taken Jim's blood pressure by pal-pation and found the level dropping. More dra-matically, Jim's heart rhythm had become more erratic. George's concentration locked onto her task again and she reached for the drug kit. Mike nodded as she held up ampoules of atropine and lignocaine. Jim's heart rate had dropped to a rate below fifty beats per minute and the extra beats being produced were joining into short runs of three or more at a time. If they couldn't control the arrhythmia with medication they could well find themselves having to put down in a field to deal with re-suscitation from a full cardiac arrest.

George administered a dose of atropine and then repeated it a minute later. An increase in heart rate might be enough to abolish the erratic beats. A third dose brought the heart rate up but didn't control the abnormal rhythm so George drew up a dose of lignocaine. The next few minutes were tense as the paramedics monitored their patient. Another dose of lignocaine was administered as they flew over the outer suburbs of the city. No chance to put down now. If Jim arrested they would have to defibrillate in flight, which was a scenario George always found nerve-racking.

Fortunately, it wasn't necessary this time. George was relieved at the speed with which Jack Burgess landed the helicopter on the painted pad of the flat expanse of the hospital roof. Having been in radio contact with Mike, members of the resuscitation team from the emergency department were waiting and Jim was whisked off to the facilities he needed most right now. George and Mike were left standing in the sunshine beside the helicopter. Jack had shut down the engines and he climbed out of the machine as the rotors made their final, slow revolutions.

'Time for coffee?' he suggested. 'Or shall we head back to base?'

'We'd better wait for our stretcher. We haven't got a spare one here at present. Coffee sounds like a good idea,' Mike decided.

'I'll pass,' George told the men. 'I might go down to the orthopaedic ward.' She eased her helmet off and tucked it under her arm. 'I'd like to check up on the chap we brought out from Arthur's Pass yesterday.'

'The doctor?' Jack looked interested. 'I heard he'd set his own leg with a couple of branches.'

'Not quite. He had another doctor with him. It was his mate that did the splinting. Good job, too,' George added. 'I didn't need to touch the alignment.'

'Must have been an easy night for you.' Mike grinned. 'With two doctors to cope with the medical side.'

George grunted, shaking her head as she walked towards the entrance leading to the lift. 'Easy' wasn't the word she would have chosen.

No way.

Nothing had changed.

And yet everything had changed.

John Maxwell had not anticipated the overwhelming assault on his emotions that a return to New Zealand would entail. It was only a brief visit after all—a three-week holiday that had been impetuously booked thanks to Dougal's insistent encouragement backed by the nostalgia his correspondence had stirred with references to old and familiar places and people.

The first jolt had come the instant he'd stepped outside the terminal building at Christchurch airport. The clarity of the air, the warmth of the spring sunshine, children wearing shorts and sandals, even the motley collection of widely varying cars and vans that had been competing for slots in the taxi ranks. Max had been unprepared for the clutch of realisation. He was *home*. He'd only become aware of the unconscious smile that had lightened his features as he'd begun to wonder why everyone he'd passed had been smiling at him.

Dougal had arranged the first week of his holiday. Being wildly enthusiastic about hiking, his friend was revelling in the unparalleled opportunities New Zealand provided. The bookshelf of his central city apartment was littered with information and maps of all the major tramping routes the country had to offer. Max had been only too happy to go along with the plan to walk from the Andrews River to Aickens, traversing the Arthur's Pass National Park from one end to the other. He had needed a few days' break from the city already, a bit of distance from the familiarity that was seducing him into thinking his new life was just an interlude.

No wonder it had been a difficult adjustment, relocating his life and career to Glasgow, Scotland. It had taken well over a year to become accustomed to the greyness of the city and the suspicious attitude of the local population who had initially assumed from his accent that he was English. His friendship with Dougal Donaldson had been largely responsible for his eventual assimilation. Dougal's enthusiasm for everything, including the outdoors, was contagious. Dougal blamed Max for his decision to try a working holiday in New Zealand. Now Max could blame Dougal for dragging him back and shaking his conviction that he had, in fact, done the right thing in emigrating.

And Max was badly shaken. The sense of being home had been disturbing but it couldn't compare with the shock of meeting Georgina Collins again. The extraordinary coincidences fate was capable of providing were unbelievable. But maybe it hadn't been that much of a coincidence. New Zealand was a small country. George had made history by becoming the first female helicopter paramedic. Tramping accidents happened all the time. Perhaps their reunion had been inevitable.

As inevitable as having to admit that no one had or could ever affect him the way George did. That gut-wrenching moment of recognition had been far more telling than the years of momentary but frequent thoughts of her. Thoughts that had ranged between physical desire, grief at the loss and anger over the bitter way they had parted. The only defence Max had been able to summon to deal with the situation of meeting her again had been to resurrect the anger. And George had helped considerably—taking charge and bossing him about, being bitchy about Rowena. And as for dragging up that reference to meat loaf! How petty could anyone get?

It wasn't helping that Dougal had fallen for George like a ton of bricks. If his friend made even one more comment about how gorgeous, talented, courageous and desirable Georgina Collins was then Max would lose it. Two days of visiting hours laced with such statements were more than enough. Max strode towards the orthopaedic ward in Christchurch hospital with resolution. He simply wasn't going to put up with any more of it. George wasn't interested. She had told him so herself. It was high time to enlighten his mate before these fantasies got out of hand.

But maybe it was too late. Dougal Donaldson's face radiated happiness when Max arrived in his private room. Propped up against pillows, with his leg suspended in a canvas sling, Dougal looked as though life couldn't be better.

'I had a visitor,' he told Max. Hazel eyes gleamed with satisfaction under the thatch of sandy hair. 'George came to see me. *Me!*' Dougal's grin was triumphant.

Max dumped the bag containing items Dougal had requested from the apartment. He turned the narrow chair back to front and straddled it, resting his arms on the back. 'Did she, now?'

'Aye.' Dougal sighed contentedly. 'She said she had a minute or two to spare after bringing a patient into Emergency so she thought she'd come and see how I was getting on, but I reckon she's just shy. She doesn't want to let on that she fancies me.'

'George is not shy, Dougal,' Max stated evenly.

'No.' Dougal looked thoughtful. 'George is perfect, that's what she is.'

'Nobody's perfect, mate,' Max contradicted.

'I've never met a woman like George before.' Dougal shook his head. 'She's such a wee thing but she's so determined.'

'Stubborn,' Max suggested.

'Strong,' Dougal amended. 'I can just imagine her as a wee bairn, fighting not to let her family make her into something she didn't want to be. She must have had a tough time.'

'You've only heard one side of that story.' Max shook his head. 'George's family all adore her. They weren't trying to stifle her personality. They were trying to put her on a pedestal.'

'One that she didn't want—with frills.'

'George's mother was a bit old school, I guess,' Max admitted. 'She found supporting her husband and raising her family gave her all the happiness she needed. She thought George could be just as happy following her example. And she was trying to keep her safe,' Max added. 'George's activities can be hair-raising for anyone who loves her to stand by and watch.'

'Maybe she just needs someone to put her on the right kind of pedestal,' Dougal suggested.

'One with rotors?' Max grinned. 'He'd have to stand back and watch it vanish into the distance.'

'Ah, but it would come back.' Dougal nodded sagely. 'The only way to truly tame a wild spirit is to give it freedom. The freedom to make its own choices.'

'George does that all right,' Max muttered. 'Always has. Always will.'

'I'm going to ask her out.' Dougal was giving Max a very determined glance.

'She won't go.'

'No harm in trying.'

'Yes, there is.' Max was having difficulty keeping his tone impersonal.

'Why?'

'She's not the right woman for you, Dougal.'

'How can you be so sure of that?'

The two men stared at each other. The silence was heavy with potential tension. Max couldn't stop Dougal pursuing George if he decided to but they both knew it would put their friendship in jeopardy.

'I agree with you, actually,' Dougal said quietly. 'George isn't the right woman for me.'

Max's jaw sagged. 'Why have you been raving on about how perfect she is, then?'

'Because she is.'

Max frowned. 'Are you still on that happy juice?'

'Nope.' Dougal grinned and moved his leg within the sling. 'Virtually pain-free I am. I'm getting up on crutches later this afternoon.' His smile faded and he looked serious again. 'George *is* the perfect woman, Max. The perfect woman for *you*.'

Max said nothing.

'You're still in love with her, aren't you, mate?'

Max remained silent.

Dougal eased back on his pillows and put his hands behind his head. 'Why don't you tell me the *real* story, Max? Forget ''Spider Woman'' and how she turned you against marriage. Tell me about George. George and *you*.'

Max rubbed his chin thoughtfully. Why not? He had nothing else to do this afternoon apart from providing company for Dougal. By finally talking about it, instead of making jokes about being sucked dry by spiders, he might even be able to make sense of it all. For all his enthusiasm, cheerfulness and optimism, Dougal actually had an intelligent and rational approach to life. While he was a few years younger than Max's thirty-eight, Dougal had been through romantic disasters traumatic enough for him to have experienced the darker side of emotional involvement. Dougal ended the moment of debate.

'How did you meet?' he demanded.

'In the emergency department,' Max told him obligingly. 'She was a junior ambulance officer. I was an anaesthetic registrar. I'd been called in to intubate a patient but the department was short-staffed when we got an influx of cases from a big MVA. It was chaos for a while. George ended up assisting me to do a chest decompression and then managing a cardiac arrest.'

'Successful?'

'Eventually. We didn't know it would be until he'd been in Theatre for hours. George came back later when we were both off duty. I offered her a coffee and we sat in the staff-room, talking, until the early hours.'

'Love at first sight, yes?'

'More like a fascination with each other and with emergency medicine. Not long after that I switched from anaesthetics to the emergency department. I'd found where I really wanted my career to go. George and I ended up having a lot of patients in common. We never seemed to get enough time to finish discussing them so we moved in together.'

'A need for professional discussions being the only motivation, I suppose.' Dougal's smile was knowing.

'We were madly in love with each other,' Max confessed. 'And George had been looking for a new property to rent. One with a bit of land because the grazing she had available for her horse was being sold off for a subdivision.'

'So you found the mansion in the country?'

'God, it was an amazing place.' Max was staring at the wall above Dougal's head, lost in reminiscence. 'Originally it was the homestead of a huge farm. By then it down to a few acres. An overgrown orchard, fantastic old stables, derelict farm sheds and equipment everywhere, and the most amazing sense of peacefulness. It was like stepping off the planet, arriving home after a shift at work. I think I could have spent the rest of my life there quite happily. George felt the same way.'

'How old were you?'

'I was thirty. George was twenty-seven.'

'How long did you live together?'

'Three years.'

'Why didn't you get married?'

'We intended to.' Max sighed. 'We were engaged by the time we moved out to the country. There just always seemed to be a reason to put the date of the wedding off. George wanted to get the exams for her intermediate qualifications out of the way. Then I was studying for my Fellowship. Then George decided to do the paramedic course. We were both so focused on our careers and, of course, the arguments had started by then.'

'What did you argue about?'

Max shrugged. The subjects didn't seem remotely important now. 'Housework not being done, no food in the house. Me cooking meat loaf too often. She thought I was just like her father and brothers—expecting the woman to do all the domestic work.'

'And were you?'

'Of course not,' Max said indignantly. 'I worked longer shifts than George did. And I didn't know *how* to cook.'

'I can't believe you broke up over meat loaf.'

'There were other problems,' Max conceded. 'We had an argument every time George got her hair cut. I just couldn't persuade her to let it grow a bit.'

'Fair enough, too,' Donald admonished. 'I wouldn't want anyone telling me how to wear my hair.'

'We had rows about her job as well.' Having started, Max was going to get it all over with.

'Why?'

'It was bloody dangerous at times. An officer got killed at that time. Struck by a vehicle when she was attending a smash on the motorway. It shook me up. Just before that, George came home with a black eye after being called to deal with an assault in a pub.'

'Happened to me once, in the emergency department.'

'The final straw was when George applied for a position at the helicopter base. I'd just read about the position in Glasgow becoming available. Emergency medicine was a new specialty in those days. I had to go somewhere where I could get some experience. I wanted

George to come with me—for us to get married, finally.'

'And she didn't want to go.' Dougal's tone made his words a statement rather than a question.

'It was more complicated than that.' Max sighed. He'd had enough of revisiting the past and wasn't sure he was liking his own part in it. 'George decided I was trying to box her in. Wanting to turn her into a wife and mother.'

'Doesn't she want kids?' Dougal sounded disappointed.

'She said she did but just not then.' Max had to smile, albeit wryly. 'She reckoned she'd hit the snooze button on her biological clock and it wasn't due to go off again for at least five years.'

'And how long ago was that?'

Max shrugged. 'Five years, I guess.'

'So—there you go.' Dougal sat up straighter, looking interested. 'Now's your chance.'

'For what?'

'Trying again. The alarm's due to go off.'

Max shook his head. 'Forget it, mate. I think she hit the button so hard she broke it.

Anyway, there's way too much emotional baggage lying around. I'm only here for another two weeks. I doubt I could even talk her into having a cup of coffee with me, let alone kids.'

Dougal's eyes narrowed. 'Why do you think she's so anti?'

'She hates me.'

'Hate's a very strong emotion. You have to be really bothered by someone to hate them. Maybe it's a cover.'

'For what?'

'The fact that she's still in love with you. Just like you are with her.'

Max snorted dubiously. 'It's a good cover. I suspect it would take a lot longer than two weeks to crack it.'

'Ah!' Dougal held up a forefinger. 'I have the solution to that problem.'

'Oh?' Max was smiling at Dougal's calculating expression.

Dougal pointed at his leg. 'See this?'

'Can't miss it, mate. It's not a pretty sight.'

'I'm out of action for about three months. On sick leave. Out of a job.'

Max nodded sympathetically. 'I imagined you would be. I'm sorry about that.'

'I was, too, until I realised the potential of the situation.'

'Which is?'

'They have to employ a locum registrar to cover me in the emergency department.'

'And?' Max could finally see where Dougal's conversation was leading. 'Hey, no way, mate. I'm here on a holiday. I'm going home in a fortnight.'

'So have a working holiday,' Dougal grinned. 'And stop talking about going home, Max. You *are* home.'

CHAPTER FOUR

THE time warp was surreal.

What the hell was John Maxwell doing in the emergency department of Christchurch hospital? It gave George the sense of having stepped back more than eight years in time. To when she'd been a junior ambulance officer, part of a road-based crew, still starry-eyed about her career and where she was going to go with it. And Max had been an anaesthetic registrar she'd never seen before, although members of that department had often been called into Emergency to help intubate and ventilate critically ill patients. George had noticed him instantly, despite the chaos caused by the sudden influx of accident victims from the bus versus bridge incident.

That blaze of white hair had been what had caught her eye initially. George had decided it had been a blond streak, deliberately engineered by someone inclined to be a trendsetter or wanting to be noticed. By women, no doubt.

George had dismissed his desirability with customarily swift decisiveness. The man hadn't needed anything extra in the physical department to catch a woman's eye so if he'd felt compelled to alter his appearance in such a dramatic fashion he'd probably been trying to deflect attention from some unattractive personality defect.

Not that George had more than a second or two to make the harsh judgement. Emergency was overloaded. She was in a queue of three stretchers bearing patients, all waiting for triage. The young man she was transporting had a chest injury. It hadn't appeared too serious on scene—probable fractured ribs, but the internal damage from sharp bone ends had clearly been building. Air or blood was accumulating somewhere in the chest cavity where it had no right to be. The patient became very distressed very quickly and George had to shout to get some attention.

'I need some help here.' She was calm but assertive. 'Now!'

It was John Maxwell that came to her assistance. They moved the stretcher into an already occupied resuscitation area, forcing staff to allow them room. George stayed with her patient and suddenly found herself assisting Max.

'Find a chest drain kit,' he instructed her.

There was no one else to help. The staff immediately surrounding them were dealing with a cardiac arrest. In the neighbouring resus area they had a child with a serious head injury. Resus 3, directly opposite, had a partial amputation with severe arterial bleeding. George didn't hesitate. She found the chest drain kit and stood by as Max confidently inserted the cannula to decompress their patient's chest.

It wasn't a tension pneumothorax causing the collapsed lung and breathing crisis. The young man's chest was collecting blood and his condition continued to deteriorate. George had to work hard from that point. She attached leads for a portable heart monitor, took blood pressure and other vital sign recordings and moved quickly to find a fresh portable oxygen cylinder. They were working in an impossibly cramped situation, trying to share facilities and equipment, with their patient on the narrow and unsuitable ambulance stretcher, but to-

gether they managed, dealing even with a resuscitation from a cardiac arrest and the ensuing intubation and ventilation of their
patient.

They took him to Theatre together and much
later, when George was off duty, she went
back to Emergency to try and find out the out-
come of the case. She searched for, and found,
John Maxwell in the staffroom. He had his feet
up on the coffee-table and looked totally exhausted.

'You're still on duty!' George was astonished.

'Not officially.' Max smiled wearily. 'Actually, I finished at 6 p.m.'

'So did I.'

They both glanced at the wall clock, now
reading nearly 11 p.m. They looked at each
other. And smiled.

'How's our young man doing, do you
know?'

'Doing well, considering. Still alive, anyway. He had a lacerated left ventricle.'

'Wow!' George hadn't realised the injury
had been so critical. 'He's been lucky, then.'

'Yeah. Lucky that I had you to help.' Max was generous in his appreciation. 'You were fantastic. Are you going to tell me your name? I'm Max, by the way.'

'I'm George.'

'George?' Max digested this information with interest. 'What kind of name is that for a girl?'

George eyed him levelly. She ignored the query. 'Tell me, Max. Why do you bleach that bit of your hair like that?'

He didn't, of course. The streak was quite natural. In fact, Max had tried to disguise it by dyeing it black at one point but the white roots had looked even more peculiar so he had abandoned the attempt. It was still just as obvious, eight years on, despite the sprinkling of grey hairs over the rest of his head. Clean-shaven again now, Max didn't really appear to have aged at all. His face was a little leaner maybe and the lines around his eyes more deeply etched, but the smile was the same. The quiet but commanding physical presence hadn't changed and the gentle scrutiny from those black eyes was just as unsettling as they had been the first time George had found them seriously assessing her as a woman and not an emergency assistant. But why was he staring at her now? What was he doing in the emergency department with a stethoscope slung around his neck, chatting to staff and patients as though his five-year period of absence had merely been a longer-than-usual holiday?

There was no opportunity to find an answer even though it was Max that accompanied the triage nurse to receive her patient.

'This is the hypothermia case?' Max began by confirming the information they had already received by radio. 'Fourteen-year-old girl?'

George nodded. 'This is Kelly Jamieson. She was on a school camp rafting expedition. She fell overboard and was washed away. Luckily she got caught in some tree branches near a small island and was able to keep her head out of the water, but it was nearly an hour before a jet boat was able to get in and rescue her.'

Kelly was wrapped in a foil blanket. She had a head covering of the same material. An IV line ran into one arm. Her eyes were closed and her skin extremely pale. Max leaned over the stretcher and touched the girl's cheek.

'Hello, Kelly? Can you open your eyes for me?'

The teenager was able to comply with the request but it was clearly an effort. Her eyes closed again before she responded verbally to Max.

'We've got Resus 1 set up,' he told George. 'With warmed saline ready to go.'

They moved quickly. Max stayed on George's side of the stretcher. 'What was the GCS when you arrived?'

'She was alert but very disoriented. Seemed like the vestiges of a state of panic, really. We landed just as the jet boat was coming in. She was still shivering at that point but stopped even before we could get her wet clothing off. Her GCS dropped rapidly. Heart and respiration rate also dropped. Our first baseline recordings showed a GCS of 10, heart rate of 55, respiration rate of 12 and a blood pressure of 80 over 50.' George checked her watch. 'That was thirty minutes ago.'

'Temperature at that point?'

'Thirty-two degrees centigrade.'

They were ready to transfer Kelly onto the bed. 'On the count of three,' Max directed. 'One, two...three.'

The transfer was smooth. The nursing staff were moving in to change the monitor leads and apply the automatic blood-pressure cuff.

'Keep that oxygen running at fifteen litres a minute with the non-rebreather mask,' Max instructed. 'Let's get the first unit of warmed saline going.'

George stepped back. This wasn't eight years ago. There were plenty of staff to assist Max. And she wasn't a junior ambulance officer. She was a paramedic. As highly qualified as she could get. She wasn't even road crew any longer. She wore the overalls and badges that advertised her unique position as the only female in the helicopter rescue team. A uniform she was normally proud to be seen in. At this moment of time, however, it felt like a placard—announcing to the world in general, and John Maxwell in particular, all the reasons why their relationship had been such a miserable failure.

Before leaving the department, George stopped to have a word with one of the consultants.

'What's John Maxwell doing here, Susan? I thought he was only in Christchurch on holiday.'

'He was.' Susan Scott smiled. 'He came over to visit Dougal Donaldson. They took a tramping trip that ended rather disastrously.'

'I know,' George told her. 'I did that mission.'

'Well, you'll know that Dougal is likely to be out of action for a fair while. We needed a locum. Having Max step in was Dougal's idea, but management was delighted. He's perfect.'

'Is he?' George eyed Susan speculatively. The consultant was probably in her early forties but she didn't look it. And she was single, not to mention rather attractive.

'Absolutely.' Susan nodded with enthusiasm. 'He's probably more qualified than anyone else here now, with all the postgraduate training and experience he's had overseas. And he didn't need to worry about work permits or anything. In fact, he used to work here.'

'I know,' George said bleakly. Having started work in the emergency department well after Max had left, Susan would have no idea of her own past relationship with the new locum.

'Dougal's been given up to three months of sick leave if he needs it,' Susan continued. 'We're hoping Max will stay at least that long. He's a really nice guy,' she added with a smile. 'The people who knew him years ago are delighted to see him back. He seems to have been really missed.'

George merely returned the smile by way of a response before moving on. The day had been quiet and this mission, the only one, had come close to the end of her shift. It was unlikely that she would return to the emergency department today so she would have time to consider how to deal with a new professional relationship with Max. Time to think about how it affected her on a personal level. Time to wonder whether she was one of the people who had really missed John Maxwell.

The southerly blast that had disrupted the rescue mission to Arthur's Pass was history. Over the four days off George had had since visiting Dougal, the weather had settled into a glorious foretaste of the summer to come. There were no late calls following the case of hypothermia and George had discarded her overalls gratefully on arriving home, changing into shorts and a light cotton knit top. The phone rang the moment she finished changing her clothes.

'Oh, I'm so sorry, Ken.' George found herself apologising to her nearest neighbour. 'I hope he hasn't done any serious damage.'

She listened for another minute, then replaced the receiver with a sigh. How on earth had Jacob managed to escape this time? And why did he have to make a beeline for Ken Stringer's prized vegetable garden? George laced some old, comfortable trainers to her feet. The Stringers lived at least a mile up the road and the verge was rough going at times. Jacob had a deep-set aversion to walking on tarmac and a stubborn streak that often made her wonder whether he was more mule than donkey. George also collected a few slices of brown bread—a treat almost guaranteed to promote co-operation.

The stable block was at right angles to the house, past the walled vegetable garden and bordering the old orchard. The gate to her own edible garden was still secure and George debated whether to dig up some carrots for Ken. She sighed again. The problem wasn't that Jacob had eaten his carrots. The small, shaggy donkey had simply cleaned off the green tops. The vegetables would still be perfectly edible. They just couldn't be entered in the upcoming A and P show.

George ducked into the shade of the stables. The stone building had been soaking in the warmth of the sunshine all day and the air was heavy, laced with the scents of hay and large, hairy animals. She reached up to take a halter and lead rope from a hook on the wall. With a sudden inspiration, George also picked up a much larger halter. Maybe she could save herself the long, hot walk.

The gate to the stable paddock was open— clear evidence that the escape should have been preventable. Had someone been onto the property and undone the complicated latch system George had devised specifically to deter the clever donkey? A quick glance at the chewed and shredded wood around the latch dispelled the worry. Jacob had managed this entirely alone. And Sylvester, bless him, hadn't budged from the paddock despite the open invitation. The geriatric black and white Clydesdale George had adopted three years ago stood with his head down, more than half-asleep in the evening warmth.

George planted a kiss on the enormous nose. 'What do you reckon, old man? Do you want to come with me to spring your wicked friend?'

Sylvester rubbed his head down the centre of George's chest. She staggered under the affectionate gesture and smiled. She had never regretted offering a home to the retired horse. The huge, gentle animal imparted a sense of peace that she appreciated intensely at times. And this was definitely one of those times.

The pace was slow, the broad, bare back as comfortable as an old armchair. Sylvester didn't need a bridle. He was quite happy to follow the direction of George's legs and voice. They ambled up the long, tree-lined driveway and Sylvester calmly gave the tethered goat near the letterbox a wide berth. Torpedo hadn't been named for the speed of his thought processes. The large, white goat had been unloaded onto George by more distant neighbours who'd found themselves unwilling to continue living with their mobile lawnmower's nasty tendency to put his head down and charge anybody who came within range.

Only one living creature enjoyed a close relationship with Torpedo and that was the cat that had strayed onto the property over two years ago. Doorstop was the ugliest cat George had ever seen but he had clearly made his mind up about where he wanted to live. When a choice was made, the large cat was not to be moved. His habit of refusing to move when George needed to close a door had led to his name. When he wasn't blocking doorways, the cat could usually be found near Torpedo, or fast asleep on Sylvester's broad rump. Right now, the oddly mottled ginger and brown cat with the bright pink nose was sitting on top of the letterbox. Doorstop reached out a lazy paw by way of greeting the horse as he carried George out onto the road.

There was no traffic. The sun was taking its time to dip below the horizon. The only sound was the clop of Sylvester's impressive hooves on the road. George's body was completely relaxed, lulled by the rocking movement of the horse. Her mind, however, had no intention of following suit.

How on earth was she going to cope with constant reminders of her past relationship with Max? She didn't need any more time to analyse the effect of his return. That sleepless night and then her days off had provided quite enough of an opportunity to find her way through the emotional maze.

There was no doubt at all left about why George had never found anyone to take John Maxwell's place in her life. She never would—because Max was the only man she had or could ever love to that extent. She recognised that now with blinding clarity. Why couldn't she have been as smart as Ted Scott and recognised the significance of what they'd had while they'd still had it? George wanted more than just the right partner for life. She wanted a child as well. The desire had always been there but had been easy enough to dampen, even when dealing with cases involving babies such as the premature twins only last week. It was something relegated to the future. Something that would be deferred until she found a partner. George didn't want just anybody's child. The father of her baby would have to be somebody she loved, preferably enough to spend the rest of her life with him. And there was only one person in existence who could fill that role. No, George didn't want just anybody's baby. She wanted Max's baby.

The knot in George's abdomen caused a tension that even Sylvester could feel. He stopped his plodding and swung his head around to stare at his mistress. George clicked her tongue reassuringly. At least the horse couldn't quite read her mind and wouldn't understand if he could. If it hadn't been George who had winched Max up to the helicopter in the nappy harness last week, she might have been spared the reawakening that the intimate body contact had provoked. Fortunately, the exercise had been swift. Hopefully too swift for Max to have any idea of the effect the contact might have had and the totally unprofessional thoughts threatening to distract George's concentration on a dangerous manoeuvre.

The acrimony with which they had parted seemed insignificant now. It was an effort to recreate the bitterness they had built between them but George had to make the effort. How else could she hope to cope over the next few weeks or however long Max ended up intruding into the orbit of her professional life?

The decision to fill in the locum position to cover Dougal's absence from the emergency department had been a surprisingly easy one to make. After nearly a week of being part of the staff, Max had to admit he was loving it. Shutting the front door of Dougal's central city apartment behind him, Max was still thinking about his day in the emergency department as he deposited the flat box containing a large Supreme Pizza onto the kitchen bench.

The work was varied and interesting, the staff great fun to work with, his expertise respected and appreciated...and he had seen George in the department on three separate occasions. While the contact with his ex-fiancée created an instant tension, Max welcomed the emotional disturbance. He knew that much of the reaction was due to a purely physical excitement—an attraction that was instantaneous and far more powerful than he had ever felt towards any other woman in his life.

Max opened the box but hardly registered the appetising burst of savoury steam that met his nose. He extracted a slice of pizza and took a large bite. The action was mechanical. His mind was still firmly elsewhere. Thank God that winching exercise had been so brief...and terrifying. Even a few more seconds of being harnessed to George with their lower bodies in such intimate contact and there would have been no hope of hiding the fact that his desire could easily have overcome the terror.

Max wanted Georgina Collins. Badly. But not badly enough to scramble his brains completely. Max knew that the other part of his reaction every time he saw George had nothing to do with sex. The feeling had caught him by surprise the first time but he was used to it now. Relief. Relief to realise that his ability to love a woman enough to make his own desires seem insignificant hadn't died along with their relationship. No one else had even come close. Rowena was a friend, nothing more, and she had wanted nothing more from him. It had been a relationship of convenience. A human contact and means to fulfil physical needs by two people who had known that their careers took precedence over anything else in their lives.

The relief was overlaid, however, by a more worrying emotion. Fear. Fear that if he let George go this time, he would have to spend the rest of his life with the knowledge that he would never find anyone else who could make him feel the way she did. Max had finished his first slice of pizza by the time he had unearthed a plate. He loaded it with another few slices.

He couldn't afford to fail this time but it was going to take a careful approach. He had to figure out what mistakes he'd made—how to rectify them and how not to make them again. Was Dougal right? Had Max attempted to make George into something she didn't want to be? Had she relegated him to the ranks of men like her father and brothers—someone she loved but had to struggle with in order to be her own person?

Carrying his plate of pizza, Max slid open the ranchslider door he had been gazing through without focus. The door led from the tidy open-plan kitchen, dining and sitting area of Dougal's small townhouse into a tiny court-yard garden. No blade of grass had attempted to establish itself in the cracks of the paving but a strip of garden containing hardy shrubs such as flax and hebes provided a smidgen of greenery. The deckchair was a more inviting place to sit and eat during the warm evening than the confines of the apartment.

Max sat down on the deckchair with a sigh. Dougal *was* right. Hadn't George said as much during the first real argument they'd ever had? Max had been so appalled when she'd come home that night sporting a black eye. The assault case her crew had been sent to deal with hadn't been contained effectively enough by the police they'd been backing up. A new fight had broken out between their patients and George had been caught right in the middle. Max's imagination had run wild. He'd listed all the dangerous situations that George's job could land her in. The list had been long. Having changed to working in the emergency department, Max had known how many violent or disturbed people got picked up in the streets. He'd known about industrial accidents and the dangers associated with attending MVAs. He hadn't wanted George near any of them. She had become progressively more angry. He was as bad as her family, she'd announced eventually—so sure about what girls should or shouldn't do.

Max had apologised. He'd told her he was worried simply because he cared so much. He'd told her she was perfect as far as he was concerned and that he loved her just the way she was. He'd asked her to marry him and George had said yes. The argument had ended with one of the most passionate nights Max had ever experienced.

They didn't set a date for the wedding. The first priority was to find somewhere to live. Somewhere that George could keep her horse. Somewhere they could be together and enjoy every limited hour that their respective careers could allow them to have together. They found that amazing property. The crumbling old, stone mansion and its acres of land. Even settled into the house and loving every minute of being together, they didn't set a date. George was focused on her upcoming courses and examinations for her Grade III qualifications. Then Max started his own study programme for a fellowship in the newly recognised specialty of emergency medicine. By the time he had been successful, George had the new goal of gaining her paramedic qualification.

Max closed his eyes. He hadn't even tasted his second slice of pizza but his appetite had gone. Daylight was fading rapidly now and the short-sleeved casual shirt he had tucked into his jeans was no longer warm enough but he didn't want to move. He had reached the crux of the problem now. The time when things had started to go wrong. But how had things escalated so swiftly? And so disastrously? The arguments seemed minor in retrospect. Housework not done—usually by Max, but he'd been quick to notice any similar failing on George's part. He'd never been able to bite his tongue when George had had her hair cut either, not when it had seemed that she'd always had it shorn off when she'd been starting to look even more beautiful than he'd thought possible. And George had hated his cooking. The cry of 'Not meat loaf *again*!' rang in his memory. It had been a joke for a long time— the only meal Max had been capable of providing. When had it turned from being a joke into a major failing and why hadn't he made an effort to improve?

Then the real trouble had started. George had learned of the upcoming paramedic position at the helicopter rescue base. She had been aglow with the dream of becoming the first woman to be successful. Max had learned of the emergency medicine consultancy available at the Royal Infirmary in Glasgow and had been just as excited at the dream of becoming a recognised expert in the new field. He should have told George when he'd applied for the position but he hadn't expected success. Or that George would be successful in her own application.

That was the showdown. The beginning of the end. Max wanted George to finally marry him and go to Scotland. His future career could depend on such a move and who was going to be the breadwinner when they decided it was time for children? But George was unwilling to give up her own opportunity. She wanted the chance to prove she could do it. They both fired the accusation that the other's career meant more than their feelings for each other.

Max denied it with perfect sincerity. If he'd thought it would have fixed the situation he would have stayed but they both knew that the frustration of throwing away the advancement to his career would engender a damaging resentment. The arguments became more bitter. George wasn't going to follow her mother's ideal of womanhood. To become a second-class citizen whose own needs had to be suppressed in favour of supporting the man in her life. They both claimed that their careers were an important part of who they were. George stated that Max would stay if he really wanted her. Max stated with equal anger that George would go with him if she really wanted him. And George's response was that she didn't.

He walked out at that point. Packed a bag, walked away from George and took the next available flight to Scotland. The bitterness was quite sufficient to prevent acting on any impulse to contact George again. It could never have worked. They were pulling in different directions and the test of strength they had just suffered demonstrated an equality that could never allow for one of them to win. Instead, they had both lost. Did George recognise the enormity of what they *had* lost?

Was there some way they could use their strength to build something together again without later tearing it apart? Max wouldn't want to go through that emotional trauma again. He couldn't afford to. If he played his cards right, surely they could both win. The chill finally forced Max to go back inside. He walked with a determined step, eating cold pizza as he went. Max felt hungry again. And confident. He was going to win this time. And so was George.

Max simply wasn't going to allow any other option.

CHAPTER FIVE

'How severe is this pain?'

'Varies a lot. Depends on what I've been doing.'

'Any sciatica?'

'A bit. Right-sided.'

'That figures.' The orthopaedic surgeon turned his gaze back to the wall of X-ray viewing screens. MRI scan images made an impressive array. He shook his head. 'I suppose you're still out there—lifting heavy loads and dangling off winching cables.'

'Mmm.'

The middle-aged surgeon, Maurice Baxter, smiled at his patient. The head shake this time conveyed admiration. 'You're an amazing woman, George. Nobody expected you to regain full mobility after your accident, let alone go back to your job.'

'My job is my life,' George said a little sadly. 'I couldn't think of another option.'

Maurice's tone was gentle. 'You may have to, George. Sooner or later. The later you leave it, the more likely it is that you're going to have to consider some more surgical intervention.'

George scanned the X-ray screens again herself. 'I can't argue with that sort of evidence. I guess I wasn't really aware of how much residual damage to the discs I would be left with.'

'It was a serious injury. We all told you that at the time but you refused to believe it. As I said, it's remarkable that you're doing what you do now. I'm certainly not surprised that you're having some problems.'

'But the sooner I stop doing it, the longer my back will hold out, yes?'

Maurice nodded. 'That's about the size of it, I'm afraid.'

A short silence ensued as the surgeon allowed George time to consider the implications of the lengthy consultation they had just finished in which they had discussed the results of the MRI scan. Maurice hadn't tried to simplify the medical information he had imparted. Neither had he spared George from his honest opinion of her prognosis. He respected George's intelligence and greatly admired her determination. While he couldn't understand how her career could mean more to her than her health, he also respected her right to make her own choices. Maurice Baxter was prepared to go out of his way to help this particular patient of his in any way he could. He waited patiently now, although the awareness of a waiting room full of outpatients anticipating a start to his afternoon clinic was becoming more noticeable.

'What would happen if I became pregnant?'

Maurice Baxter was genuinely startled. Then he wondered why the idea was so unexpected. Georgina Collins was a talented and very attractive young woman. There must be any number of men who would vie for a position as her partner. In the three years Maurice had known George, however, a partner or a family had never been hinted at in his patient's determined plans for her future. He found a smile creeping over his face.

'I expect you'd end up having a baby,' Maurice told George.

His patient grinned and rolled her eyes. 'You know what I meant. How would it affect my back?'

Maurice became serious. 'You might get pretty uncomfortable in the later stages of pregnancy. You'd have to be careful. The extra weight being carried and a change of posture would mean further strain on your back, which would carry some risk. I'd want to keep a close eye on you but I certainly wouldn't advise against it.' The smile returned. 'Are you planning on getting pregnant, George?'

'No. I was just curious.' George's gaze was now on the clock. 'I'd better go. You've given up your whole lunch-break for me, Maurice. You've got an outpatient clinic due to start, haven't you?'

'It was my pleasure, George.'

'Thanks very much. I really appreciate it.'

'Any time.' Maurice raised an eyebrow. 'Do you need a prescription for any painkillers? Anti-inflammatories?'

George shook her head. 'I'm managing. I did need to find out whether things were likely to get any worse in the near future, though.'

'They won't. Not if you start taking good care of yourself.'

'I'll do that. Thanks again, Maurice.'

'You're welcome.' Maurice watched George move towards the door of his office. 'And, George?'

She turned, her face expectant.

'Let me know when you do get pregnant.'

'I will, but it's more a case of if, not when.' George turned back to the door. 'I wouldn't hold your breath, Maurice.'

George used a phone in the emergency department to ring the communications centre. 'I've finished my appointment,' she informed them. 'Is there a road crew that might be available to take me back out to the base?'

'The chopper's on a mission,' the communications officer told George. 'Their ETA at the hospital should be about thirty minutes. I'll let Ted know you've finished and they can page you when they get there.'

'Thanks.' George hoped it hadn't been a difficult mission for one paramedic to handle. Mozzie had been adamant that he didn't want her to go through the hassle of arranging a replacement for the hour or so she had needed off for her appointment.

'Your back's important,' he told her. 'We probably won't get a job anyway.' Mozzie had driven her in to the hospital, telling her that the base truck was in need of a run. An ambulance was permanently stationed at the helicopter base. Being so close, the staff were always on standby for any emergency within the airport environs.

George decided to get herself a cup of coffee before heading up to the helipad to await the arrival of her colleagues. The emergency department was very busy so she was surprised to find Max in the staffroom.

'Can I make you a coffee?' Max was stirring a mug. He fished a teabag out with the spoon.

George smiled. 'Actually, I think I prefer the way you make tea.'

'Do you?' Max looked pleased. 'Tea it is, then. In fact, have this.' He handed her the mug. 'I'll make myself another one.'

'Got any condensed milk?' George would never forget how delicious that first cup of tea up on the mountain had been.

'Sorry. That's only available for billy-made tea.' Max slid a sideways glance towards George. 'You'll have to come and camp out with me again.'

'Maybe I will,' George responded lightly. She was trying to keep the atmosphere friendly but Max's sudden silence as he made his own drink made her feel like she had put her foot firmly in her mouth. Max seemed to be struggling to find a response.

'What have you brought in for us?' he asked eventually. The change of subject appeared deliberate.

'Nothing. I was here to see someone. I'll get picked up by the team shortly but I don't know what they're bringing in.'

'Were you visiting Dougal?'

'No.' George wasn't going to tell Max about her appointment with the surgeon. 'But that's a good idea. I haven't seen him since last week.'

'He's going to be discharged tomorrow. The surgeon's very pleased with his progress. I'm just on my way up to visit him myself.' Max took a sip of his tea. 'I'm having my first day off.'

'Who's his surgeon? Maurice Baxter?'

'Yes.' Max quirked an eyebrow. 'Do you know him?'

'He's very good,' George replied evasively. 'He's certainly the person I'd pick to operate on me.'

'I'm very impressed with the standards of specialist care,' Max told her. 'Even though I've only been here for a week.'

'Are you enjoying it?'

Max nodded, swallowing another mouthful of tea.

'Must be a bit different to Glasgow.'

'Very different. But nice.'

'Is your job in Glasgow what you wanted?' George wished she hadn't asked as soon as the words came out. It seemed to beg the question of whether the job was something he'd wanted more than he'd wanted her.

'It's a great job. I'm head of the emergency department there now.'

'I guess you'll be missing the responsibility, then.' Being a locum registrar in another city must seem like a sizeable demotion.

'Not really.' Max sounded surprised at his own admission.

'They can't have been too happy when you told them you were extending your holiday.'

'No.' Max looked thoughtful. 'In fact, I may not be very popular when I do go back.'

'I'm sure you've got lots of friends.' George watched Max rinse out his mug.

'Dougal was my best mate there and it looks like he's jumped ship. Management can be a little frustrating to deal with at times.'

'It's the same everywhere.' George tipped out the remnants of her own drink. 'I'm sure Raewyn will be delighted to see you back.'

'Who?'

'Your girlfriend. Wasn't that her name? The one who knits and looks like a horse.'

Max snorted. 'You mean Rowena. She doesn't look any more like a horse than you do, George. And she's a friend—nothing more.' Max eyed George with interest. She had never been inclined to pass comments that were bitchy. Her attitude to Rowena had smacked of jealousy from the start. While part of Max latched onto her reaction with delight, he knew it was paramount to try and clarify the situation. 'The only thing that's kept me in

Scotland this long has been my career. It has nothing to do with a woman.'

'Of course not.' George's agreement was a little too quick.

'What's that supposed to mean?'

'I mean that a woman could never compete with your career, could she?' George's question held an edge of bitterness. 'If that's what she was trying to do, I feel sorry for her.'

Max had tried to keep a lid on his irritation with George's line of conversation. He had been determined not to dredge up the past and make accusations, but his control slipped a notch now.

'Is that how you saw it, George? Did I have to give up my career in order to show you how much you meant to me? Things don't always have to be all or nothing, you know. In fact, it's kind of selfish not to contemplate an area of compromise, isn't it?'

George swallowed. He was right. She *could* have compromised. She could have gone to Scotland and continued her career. Maybe she couldn't have worked on helicopters in Glasgow but she wouldn't have had to give it all up and sit home having babies instead.

'My mother spent her whole life compromising,' George said defensively. 'She always ended up with exactly what my father and brothers wanted.'

'How is your mother?' Max asked courteously.

'She's fine.' George could still sense the anger Max was trying to control. Was the anger she felt herself genuine or was she simply absorbing Max's emotional state with the same awareness she had for everything else about him? The internal tension she could feel spreading like wildfire could be anger. It could also be the effect of trying to dampen the overwhelming physical desire sparked by standing so close to this man.

'Is she happy?'

'Yes.' George stepped away from Max. She could see where his logic was going and she didn't like it.

'Are *you* happy, George? Is your job on the helicopters what *you* really wanted?'

'Yes.' George's answer came out quickly. Too quickly. She didn't meet his gaze.

The sudden silence was heavy. George knew what Max was waiting for. He wanted her to look at him. He wanted to judge the veracity of her claim by direct eye contact. And George couldn't give it to him. If he guessed—and he would, instantly—that she was being less than truthful then she might be forced to admit that she'd been wrong. That she'd thrown away the most important thing in her life by her unreasonable determination to get what she'd thought she had to have in order to be true to herself, and therefore happy.

Suppose she *had* been selfish? It was a hard thing to admit and right now was certainly not the time or place for such a confession. Even if George could swallow her pride enough to make it, hadn't Max been just as selfish on *his* part? He had tried to change who she was because it hadn't fitted in with what he'd wanted. The emotional confusion George was left with had taken only seconds to accumulate. It was long enough for Max to reach out a hand as though he was going to touch her. To compel George to look at him and find out the truth with a searching gaze from those black eyes that had the ability to gaze at her soul.

The brief moment in time was also enough for her pager to sound, breaking the silence with a strident intrusion. Max's hand dropped to his side. George's gaze stayed down, now focused on the pager message being displayed.

'The chopper's on the roof. We've got another mission lined up. See you later, Max.'

Max watched her stride ahead of him as he left the staffroom. He followed her as far as the lift she needed to take to roof level. He planned to take the stairs to the orthopaedic ward where Dougal would be expecting him. Why wouldn't George look at him? *Was* she really happy? Did she really believe that a compromise all those years ago would have changed her life into one modelled on that of her mother—one that she had spent her life avoiding so resolutely?

Max let out a long breath. Maybe he'd never realised the significance of all those funny stories George had told him about her childhood. Like cutting off her hair, the fist fights in the playground, her amusing accounts of the ballet lessons she had loathed and the performance evening she had sabotaged single-handedly. They had taken on a somewhat different slant, hearing her talk to Dougal that night up on the mountain. Maybe she hadn't been so selfish.

Maybe fighting to prove herself had been essential to George's emotional survival.

Max could have made a compromise himself. Not going to Scotland might have slowed his career advancement but it wouldn't have been professional suicide by any means. He had been wrong. He hadn't recognised why things had gone sour. He hadn't realised he was losing the most valuable thing in his life by walking away from George. Max was quite prepared to swallow his pride and admit his error. He would be more than happy to wipe out the grievances he had fostered for so long and start again with a clean slate. One that could be written on with all the wisdom from a hard lesson well learned. The difficulty was going to be trying to find a way to make the admission. A way that George would understand and believe in.

The new mission was an MVA on a country road, not far from the small rural township of Geraldine. George strapped herself in and closed her eyes as the helicopter lifted off from the hospital roof. She needed to focus on her job and didn't want the distraction that the encounter with Max threatened to leave her with.

So Rowena was nothing more than a friend, was she? That figured. A brain surgeon probably wasn't about to give up her career to give Max the sort of home life he craved. She wasn't interested in having children anyway by the sound of it. Hadn't Dougal said something about her not knowing what a bootee would be for? Then again, Max might have given up his dreams of having a family. There must be any number of women out there who'd happily sacrifice any career ambitions to love and be loved by John Maxwell. Or at least modify those ambitions. Compromise was essential to the success of any long-term relationship. A yardstick to measure loyalty and commitment. That was where she and Max had gone wrong. And they had both been at fault. They had set themselves up in opposite corners with their expectations and ambitions.

Why had neither of them been prepared to take the first step onto middle ground? George could only answer the question for herself and she hadn't budged because she'd known that a one sided compromise could never have worked. It would have been a step onto a slippery slope of losing her own identity completely. She hadn't trusted Max enough to meet her halfway. She hadn't trusted herself enough to recognise what had really mattered.

'All right, George?' Murray sounded concerned.

'I'm fine, thanks, Mozzie.'

'What did the doc say about your back?'

George scowled faintly, waggling her hand to indicate a marginal judgement. 'I might squeeze a few more useful years out of it if I'm lucky.'

'Doesn't sound too good.'

George opened her eyes to see the empathy in Murray's expression. It held a shadow of something darker as well. Disappointment perhaps—or fear. Being forced out of their careers by physical injury or disability was something they all dreaded. The fact that 'Big George' had defied the odds and fought her way back was an inspiration to everyone on the base. To admit defeat would affect them all, and George didn't want to let her colleagues down.

'Don't worry.' George managed a smile. 'They told me I'd probably never walk again, didn't they?'

'Yeah.' Murray grinned back. 'And look at you now.'

George nodded briefly. It was time to change the subject. Time to move away from introspective agonising in emotional or physical arenas and get on with her job. They would be landing in a matter of minutes. 'What do we know about this MVA?'

'Car versus car. Head-on collision. One status zero in each of the vehicles. Three other patients. One status two, multi-trauma who's trapped in the vehicle. That's the woman we've been called for. Don't know about the others.'

George nodded again. A road-based crew must be already on scene. The fact that the accident involved fatalities meant that the potential for other victims to be seriously injured was high. The trapped woman might not be the only patient they would need to evacuate.

Ted brought the helicopter down gently, landing in a field alongside the accident scene. A fire engine and ambulance flanked the mangled cars and a small crowd of people surrounded one of the vehicles. George slung the trauma pack over the fence before holding the top wires apart to slide her body through. Murray was at her side as the group of local voluntary emergency personnel made way for them. Two fire officers were lifting a large section of crumpled metal away from the car. An ambulance officer looked relieved to notice the arrival of the paramedics.

'We haven't been able to get close enough to even get a collar on her,' she told Murray anxiously. 'She's been unconscious since we arrived.'

The noise of the generator driving the heavy cutting equipment cut off abruptly. 'We're clear,' someone called.

Murray and George were already starting their assessment. The finding of no palpable radial pulse wasn't surprising. The victim looked to be in critical condition. Severe facial injuries were contributing to the respiratory distress the woman was in. George held her head to provide stabilisation for her neck. Murray took only seconds to assess the neck and head before slipping an oxygen mask over the broken face.

'No tracheal deviation or obvious cervical deformity and the jugular veins are flat,'

Murray reported to George. 'Pupils are equal and reactive but I don't like this level of airway obstruction. Let's get a collar on her and get her out.'

The procedure to immobilise the woman's spine and remove her from the wreckage was swift thanks to the number of trained personnel on the scene. George and Murray worked fast in the clearer space. George put in a wide-bore IV line as her partner made a rapid overall assessment of their patient. The woman was seriously injured. A more detailed examination could be done *en route*. Right now they needed to ensure that her airway was patent, that she was receiving enough oxygen and that there was no major haemorrhage to be controlled.

'I'm going to intubate,' Murray told George as she opened the flow on the IV line. 'Chest movement is equal and sounds clear but the facial injuries are compromising the airway and it's only going to get worse as the swelling increases.'

George opened the kit and handed Murray the laryngoscope. She had the bag valve mask ready to attach as soon as Murray slid the endotracheal tube into position and tied it into place. With the airway secure, breathing now adequate with assistance and circulation support in place with the IV fluids running, they were ready to move their patient. They carried the woman, strapped to the backboard, to the helicopter less than ten minutes after arriving on scene.

Even during the intense period of management, Murray and George had gathered all the information they needed about their patient and the incident. The woman's name was Jennifer Lowe. A friend of the local ambulance officer, Jenny had been taking her two-year-old son to a playgroup when she'd been involved in a head-on collision with a middle-aged couple on a day trip from Christchurch. The toddler had been thrown from the car and had died instantly. In the second vehicle, the driver had also been killed instantly. His wife had multiple abrasions and fractures to one lower leg and arm but her condition was stable and she would be transported by road.

Jenny's baby had been secured in a rear-facing car seat and appeared uninjured. The ambulance officer was carrying the car seat as she followed the procession to the helicopter.

'Can you take Jenny's baby with you?' she begged George. 'Her husband works in Christchurch. He'll be meeting you at the hospital.'

George caught Murray's eye. The baby didn't appear to be injured but would need a detailed check-up, preferably by a specialist paediatrician. It would take some time to transport the infant by road and in the meantime the father would be having to deal with the situation of a critically injured wife and the loss of their older child. It might be advisable to keep what remained of the family as close together as possible. George nodded and reached for the bucket seat as fire officers helped Murray load the patient into the helicopter.

'His name's Peter,' the ambulance officer added. Tears were clearly imminent. 'He's only three weeks old.'

'I'll take care of him,' George promised. She strapped the child restraint onto her normal seat in the helicopter. She wouldn't be using it on the brief trip as all her time would be needed to help assess and monitor Jenny. Her task of assisting the young mother's breathing and keeping an eye on the cardiac monitor allowed no more than an occasional glance at the baby. The tiny face was crumpled as he cried continuously. George hoped the baby's misery wasn't due to an undiscovered injury. She wondered if the flight was hurting his ears. Maybe he was just hungry or frightened. Or both.

Murray was in contact with the emergency department by radio.

'Rescue One to Emergency. How do you read?'

'Loud and clear,' came the response. 'Over.'

'We're coming to you with a twenty-eight-year-old female, status one,' Murray reported. 'Driver of a vehicle involved in an open road, head-on MVA that included fatalities in both vehicles. She has sustained facial and abdominal injuries and a fractured femur. She is intubated and is currently receiving a second unit of saline. Heart rate is 130, respiration rate is 20 with assistance. Systolic blood pressure is 80. Do you require any further information?'

'What's your ETA, Rescue One?'

'Approximately five minutes.'

'Roger.' The line was still clear. 'We'll see you when you get here.'

The resus team waiting on the rooftop for the arrival of the helicopter didn't include Max. It wasn't until George had watched Murray take over the ventilation device and move towards the lift with the emergency staff that she remembered Max wasn't working today. He had only come in to visit Dougal. Nobody had taken any notice of their extra passenger. Peter's howls were now clearly audible as the helicopter rotors wound down. George pulled her helmet and gloves off, reaching for the safety belt inside the child restraint.

'You look like you could use a cuddle,' she told the baby. In perfect agreement, Peter hiccuped and buried his head against her shoulder. George rocked the baby and rubbed his back as his crying subsided. Ted peered into the back of the helicopter.

'Suits you,' he said with a grin. 'Are you planning to keep it?'

George shook her head. 'I'll take him downstairs. I expect his dad will be pleased to see him.'

The baby might be all that Peter's father would be left with if Jenny's condition deteriorated any further. George had witnessed many tragedies in her career but the pain they caused never ceased to move her. Life was precious. And fragile. She held the baby cradled in her arms as she made her way slowly towards the emergency department. The main desk area was empty of staff. Three resus areas had been curtained off to accommodate the influx of specialists and equipment called in to attend to Jenny. Murray was nowhere to be seen and George presumed he was observing the continuing resuscitation and possibly completing their paperwork.

She sat down on a chair that allowed her to see the screen relaying Jenny's ECG and vital signs. George was pleased to see an improvement in her patient's condition.

'Your mummy's heart rate is a bit slower and her blood pressure has gone up a bit,' she told Peter. 'That's good.'

The baby blinked, his eyes fastened on George's face. She made a clicking sound with her tongue and Peter's face became more alert, his mouth moving in what could have been either a grimace or a smile. George watched intently, repeating the sound that seemed to have pleased the infant.

'Suits you.'

The quiet voice beside George startled her. Her gaze flew up to find Max observing her.

'What are you doing out here?' George queried. 'There's a major resus in progress.'

'I'm off duty,' Max reminded her. 'And there's quite enough spectators in there already. I've just been up to visit Dougal.' He reached out and touched Peter's cheek. 'Pretty newly hatched, isn't he?'

'Only three weeks old,' George confirmed. 'But he can smile already.'

'Really?' Max hadn't taken his hand away from the baby and a tiny hand came up to grasp his finger. Max smiled delightedly. 'Look at that!' he instructed George.

George couldn't look away but it wasn't the baby's grip that caught her attention so poignantly. It was the expression on the face of Max. Would he look just like that if he was touching his own baby? Or would that tender amazement be even more pronounced? George could imagine so easily that it was Max's child she held. The strength of *wanting* it to be Max's baby in her arms was overpowering. Thank goodness the arrival of the admissions clerk broke the moment before either she or Max could get any more clucky. And thank goodness she didn't tell George that holding a baby suited her.

'Is that the Lowe baby?' she queried briskly. 'His father's in the relatives' room and there's a paediatrician expecting him. Can you take him through?'

'Sure.' George rose and Max disengaged the tiny fingers from his own. She didn't look at Max, too afraid that some remnant of her thoughts might still be visible. The moment might have been broken but the desire hadn't diminished.

Having delivered Peter, George made her way back up to the rooftop to collect the car seat, climbing each flight of stairs with a deliberate tread. You could have a baby if that was what you really wanted, she told herself. Why not? It would be the perfect way to ease herself out of her job without disappointing her colleagues by admitting physical defeat. It would give her a reason to want to be at home and would provide a future. She would know just what she would be doing in five or ten years' time. She would be being a mother which would, quite possibly, be even more fulfilling than the career she had chased and succeeded in.

By the third flight of stairs, the idea was becoming almost logical. George could afford to give up work. The house had been cheap and she was almost mortgage-free. She had been well paid over the last five years and the renovations to the property had been done largely by her own labour. Things might be a bit tight but she could start some sort of a home business for the future. With the amount of fertile land she had, the scope was endless. George could grow hazel-nut trees, or flowers for export. Exotic vegetables or herbs or even truffles. The possibilities were as exciting as the thought of having a baby.

But she didn't want just anybody's baby, she reminded herself. By the fifth and last flight of stairs, the line of George's thoughts had taken a direction that stopped her in her tracks. She leaned against the wall of the landing. Her relationship with Max might have been irreparably damaged but the physical attraction was still there in spades—at least on her part. What if she made a move to see whether Max felt the same way about her? They might have a month or two to try again. And if it still couldn't work, then maybe—if she was lucky—she might be left with something she wanted almost as much as she wanted John Maxwell.

She might have his child. The child they would have probably had by now if they had stayed together. A planned child who would be loved and nurtured. Circumstances often led to a baby being raised by only one parent. Look at how close little Peter Lowe had come to losing his mother today. It might be a less than a perfect family but it didn't have to be a major disadvantage. George would see to that. She would give her baby the best and most loving upbringing possible.

Her baby. George smiled dreamily.

Max's baby.

CHAPTER SIX

THE request for a response became more demanding.

Having sounded for the second time, the ringing of the doorbell was followed by several heavy raps from the old lion's-head doorknocker. George hastily jumped out of the shower, wrapped a towel around her body and padded damply towards the window of her upstairs bedroom. Who on earth could be pounding on her door? Her first thought was that Jacob had escaped, but everyone knew where the naughty donkey belonged. They would have telephoned.

George opened the catch on the ancient sash window and then struggled to raise the lower pane. She had painted the frames last year and some were inclined to stick rather badly. What if Jacob had strayed onto the road and caused an accident? Or someone had run over Doorstop and had had the decency to try and find the cat's owner? George shoved harder

154

and the window slid upwards with a sudden rush. She leaned out, her hair sending a cascade of drips onto the crushed shell driveway below.

The shout to attract the attention of the caller died on her lips as George caught sight of the figure standing outside her massive front entrance. She could only see his back and the top of his head but there was no mistaking that streak of white hair. How had Max discovered where she was living? And why had he come to visit—uninvited? George pulled her head back inside abruptly, reaching up to grip the edge of the window and pull it closed again. Now firmly stuck, her efforts succeeded only in dislodging the towel tucked under her arms. George could see Max turning away from the door, his gaze raking the house. She dived frantically for cover.

'Hello?' Max must have caught a glimpse of movement behind the window. Maybe he wouldn't notice the fact that the window was now wide open and would come to the conclusion that he had imagined a sign of occupation. 'Is anybody home?'

His voice became louder. He *had* noticed the window—he was standing directly beneath it. 'It's not Miss Abernethy, is it?'

George stifled a giggle at the thought of the elderly previous owner being in this predicament. As mad as the old lady had been, poor Miss Abernethy was unlikely to have ever been lying stark naked on her bedroom floor with a man trying to attract her attention.

'I'm John Maxwell,' the voice continued politely. He had certainly seen enough to be convinced that someone was at home. 'I'm sorry to disturb you but I used to live here. I was hoping to have a look around.'

George's thoughts raced. So he *didn't* know who the owner of the property now was. And he hadn't come looking for her. Perversely, George felt disappointed. Then relieved. Max would be hurt that she hadn't told him about purchasing the property they had both loved so much. He had specifically asked where she was living the night they'd met on the mountaintop and she had avoided telling him. It would be a shock if he found out by chance, having come simply with the hope of revisiting a place that he must still feel a strong connection with.

Upsetting Max wasn't something George wanted to do right now. In fact, she had spent the last several days trying to work out a way of enticing Max a little closer. It had been a frustrating exercise. During his days off, George couldn't persuade herself that even her interest in Dougal's progress was enough of a reason to make such personal contact. Dougal might get the wrong idea or even be unwilling to give her the information that would assist her in contacting Max. The one day they might have casually met in the emergency department had been the quietest day ever at the base. Not a single call. No patient to deliver to Emergency and no excuse at all to spend any time in the department. Then George had started her four days off with absolutely no opportunity for a casual encounter. Nearly a whole week wasted. Her dream was taking firmer shape all the time but it was still nothing more than a dream.

The crunch of footsteps on the crushed shells made George bite her lip. Was Max giving up? Here was the perfect opportunity she had been trying so hard to engineer and she was letting him walk away. George scrambled to her feet beside the window and cautiously tilted her head to peer outside. Max wasn't walking towards the road. He was heading for the back of the house. Perhaps he intended knocking on the kitchen door. George groaned aloud. That door would be wide open. Any minute now she might find him standing at the bottom of the staircase. She grabbed for some clothes, pulling some bike shorts from a drawer and hauling her favourite oversized old shirt from its hanger. George dragged a comb roughly through her hair and rolled up the sleeves of the faded blue shirt as she ran downstairs.

Max couldn't be allowed to leave. It was inevitable that he would find out sooner or later that George owned the property—that was, if her plan was going to go anywhere at all. She didn't want to have to find an explanation for avoiding him when she had obviously been at home. It was hardly a friendly gesture. Not the best way to start trying to re-create a relationship that might provide the means to George's new goal of sorting out her life. Racing through the kitchen and scullery, George paused by the door of the wash house to don her old pair of trainers.

The warmth and brightness of the evening sunshine struck George as she stepped outside. Shading her eyes with her hand against the glare, George scanned the immediate area but Max was nowhere to be seen. The washing she had hung out this morning hung limply in the still warmth. The ride-on lawnmower was still parked on the cobbled area. The tools she had been using to try and repair the mower were scattered around the machine exactly where she had abandoned them in favour of working off her frustration with some hard manual labour in the vegetable garden.

The yard felt deserted but then George noticed both Sylvester and Jacob moving away from the corner of their paddock shaded by the huge old elm trees. They were moving with purpose—the way they did when George went out to visit them with a slice of bread in her hand. But they weren't moving in her direction. Something—or someone—else had attracted their attention.

George watched as the incongruous pair headed towards the stables. The building had a central runway between the stalls that opened in an archway at both ends. One end was visible from their paddock. The other end led onto the driveway that ran out to the road with a branch joining the semicircle in front of the house. It was a logical path to take by someone intent on seeing more of the property. Max was inside the stable block.

Taking a deep breath, George skirted the mower and scattered tools, passed the wheelbarrow still laden with weeds from the vegetable garden and ignored the hens that had begun to congregate hopefully around her feet. She stepped into the dim light of the stables.

Max was standing at the paddock end of the block, his figure a dark silhouette against the bright background. George blinked, waiting for her eyes to adjust to the change in light. She couldn't tell whether Max was facing her or not.

'Hello, Max.' George's voice came out with a curious huskiness. She cleared her throat as she kept walking forwards.

Max was completely silent. He stood as still as a statue. As George's vision adapted she could see that he had been watching her arrival. His expression bordered on one of horror. She jumped as he suddenly closed the final distance between them and gripped her shoulders.

'Good God, you're real!' he exclaimed. An embarrassed smile twisted his mouth. 'I thought I was seeing a ghost.'

'I'm sorry I didn't answer the door. I was in the shower.'

Max released one of her shoulders, reaching up to touch her damp hair. 'So you were.' His hand settled back on her shoulder and the grip George was being held in lessened. He squeezed again, as though convincing himself of her presence, then dropped both hands and stepped back to stare at George with a puzzled frown.

'Why were you in the shower?'

'I've been slaving away in the vegetable garden all afternoon. I was hot and sweaty.' George spoke quickly, wanting to dispel a feeling of unreality she was experiencing now herself. 'Probably smelly, too.'

'No.' Max shook his head slightly. 'I mean, what were you doing in the shower…*here*?'

'I live here,' George responded simply.

'You said you'd bought a house.' Max's tone was a challenge.

'I did.' George couldn't help the proud grin that escaped. 'I bought *this* house.'

'I don't believe it!' Max looked as though someone were offering him a large lottery prize.

'Miss Abernethy died,' George explained. 'The only relatives lived in Australia. They couldn't be bothered coming here to see the place and probably thought it was an old ruin miles from anywhere. They wanted a quick sale so I got the place amazingly cheaply.'

'And you live here…alone?'

'Not exactly alone.' George bit her lip. What would Max think of her weird collection of pets? She could see Jacob and Sylvester in their paddock as she shifted her gaze to stare past Max.

'Ah.' Max had made an assumption that George didn't know quite how to address. He looked uncomfortable himself, then he cleared his throat. 'So you never moved,' he said softly. 'After I left.'

'I never wanted to move,' George said just as quietly. 'Remember?'

Max looked away and the atmosphere became instantly tense. Then his gaze slid back towards George. 'You're wearing my shirt,' he said offhandedly.

'Oh…am I?' George was genuinely surprised. She had worn this garment for so long she had quite forgotten its origin. She bit her lip. 'Do you want it back?'

'You keep it,' Max said generously. 'It looks better on you, anyway.'

Jacob had decided he'd waited long enough for their attention. He unleashed a long and demanding bray. Max's jaw dropped.

'What, in the name of heaven, is *that*?'

'My donkey.' George laughed at Max's expression. 'His name's Jacob. Come and meet him.'

Max turned and followed George the short distance to the gate opposite the stable archway. He squinted in the bright sunshine. 'You ride a donkey now?'

'No. Jacob's just a pet. I ride this chap.' George reached up to rub the side of the Clydesdale's massive head. The old horse leaned further over the fence, aiming to scratch his cheek on Max's shoulder. Max stood his ground manfully until Jacob also leaned over the fence. The donkey's neck craned as his lips delicately mouthed the pocket on the back of Max's well-worn jeans.

'He's looking for a treat,' George warned. 'Jacob—*no*!'

It was too late. Jacob had fastened his teeth onto the rim of the pocket and stepped backwards. The denim ripped, removing both the pocket and a portion of the jeans' seat. The silky-looking black underwear Max was wearing was clearly visible. Max felt the damage as he glared at the donkey. The patch of denim disappeared into Jacob's mouth and was gone in an instant.

'My God, he's a monster!'

'He does have some behavioural problems,' George admitted. 'His previous owners found him a bit difficult to live with.'

'I can believe that.' Max rubbed the spot where his pocket had been.

'He does have his good points. He's wonderful company for Sylvester.'

'Sylvester?'

'This wee fellow.' George now had the weight of the Clydesdale's head resting on her shoulder. Max's gaze travelled up the animal's impressive height.

'You *ride* him?'

'We have the occasional amble around. Sylvester doesn't go very fast any more. He's twenty-eight. I adopted him to give him a nice place to retire to.'

'Where's Minstrel?' Max glanced into the paddock as though expecting to see the fiery chestnut gelding George had once ridden.

'Long gone.' George was offhand. 'I don't do any serious riding any more. I told you that.'

'Hmm.' Max gave her a questioning glance. George ignored it.

'I've got a cat, too. And a few hens and a goat.'

'Yes—I met the goat.' Max sounded wary. 'In fact, I suspect I only got out of its way in the nick of time.'

George laughed again. 'People often send me recipes for goat stew after they've been out here for a visit.'

'I'm surprised anyone comes to visit,' Max told her. 'These animals are dangerous. Is that it? You don't have a vicious dog tucked away somewhere?'

'No, no dogs. I'd love to have one,' George said wistfully, 'but my shift hours aren't compatible with looking after a dog.'

'You said you weren't living here alone,' Max pointed out evenly.

'I was referring to the animals.'

'Oh.' Max digested this information slowly. Then he smiled at George. 'Can I see what you've done to the house?'

'Sure.'

They wandered back through the stables. The hens spotted George and clucked disapprovingly. 'They want their dinner,' she told Max. 'I'll just go and get some grain.'

By the time George had scattered the hens' food, Max's attention had been caught by the ride-on mower.

'Is there something wrong with it?'

'Yes.' George kicked the back tyre of the small tractor. 'I spent half the morning trying to fix the damned thing. I'll have to get a hay-maker in to deal with the lawns at this rate.'

'What's wrong with it?'

'It won't go.'

Max grinned. 'Don't get too technical on me here, but is there a reason *why* it won't go?'

'Probably,' George said tersely. Then she caught Max's eye and sighed resignedly. 'I have absolutely no idea why,' she confessed.

'Want me to have a look at it?'

'If you can fix it, I'll...' George tried to think of an appropriate inducement. 'I'll cook you dinner.'

'You're on.' Heedless of his clean, open-necked white shirt, Max swooped on a span-ner. As he squatted to stare at the motor, the tear on his jeans expanded. George's eyes wid-ened as more of Max's underwear became vis-ible. Luckily, Max was now intent on his task and didn't notice her fascinated gaze.

'I'll see what I've got in the fridge,' George excused herself. 'Just in case you're success-ful.'

'I'll be successful,' Max muttered. 'I'm hungry.'

George was tempted to get inside her fridge. The prospect of luring Max into her bed had gone unexpectedly from fantasy to reality and she found herself as excited as she had been during the lead-up to the first time they had ever made love. More excited even, because she knew just what Max was capable of providing in the bedroom. And George was starved for it. The hunger had been building for five years.

Five years of no man's touch or kiss being compelling enough to make her want more. George gazed sightlessly into the refrigerator. The excitement was tinged with nervousness. They had been in love then, she and Max, and maybe that had been what had created the magic in bed. She knew her feelings for Max hadn't changed but what about him? And what about the resentment for the way they had treated each other? That could be a serious barrier to overcome. George shivered. There was no need to climb inside her fridge to cool off now. Not that it would have been difficult to find space. Apart from a few cans of lager, some suspect yoghurt and an old block of cheese, her fridge was absolutely empty.

The sweet sound of the ride-on mower's engine purring happily greeted George as she went back outside. Max's clean shirt now sported smudges of grease and dirt. He dusted off his hands and sighed contentedly. 'What's for dinner?'

'Not much,' George had to admit. 'How 'bout a beer instead?'

'A beer as well,' Max corrected. 'I'm starving.'

'Um…well, actually, I haven't got very much in the fridge at the moment.'

'Really?' The ensuing silence spoke volumes. It had always been Max who had been blamed for neglecting to stock up on groceries when they'd run out of food at frequent intervals. Max checked his watch and then raised an eyebrow at George curiously. 'It's nearly 8 p.m.,' he said. 'What were you going to eat for dinner?'

'Something out of the veggie garden, I expect,' George replied. 'And maybe an egg. I hadn't really thought about it yet.'

'Salad and an omelette sounds perfect.' Max nodded. 'I'll do the omelette.' He moved away. 'I suppose the hen house is still in the same place?'

George nodded helplessly. The agenda had been taken out of her hands. Max looked back over his shoulder. 'Get going,' he instructed. 'Find a lettuce or something.'

Max eyed the donkey warily as he made his way down the side of their paddock towards the dilapidated hen house near the elm trees. The hens were following him, having noticed that dusk was imminent and that there was no more food to be had in the stable yard. Max pulled open the door of the bleached wooden shed and stooped to gain entrance to the low structure. The nesting boxes were full of clean hay but there were no eggs to be seen. Max retraced his steps slowly, having told the hens they were useless and didn't deserve to be fed if they couldn't produce a single egg in return. His verdict was half-hearted, however. The hens were a vital ingredient in the rural atmosphere of the farmyard. The soft sound of their clucking added a welcome variation to the buzzing of the insect life and the occasional contented horsy nicker from the Clydesdale. Max paused by the gate near the stables.

This was heaven on earth, this place. Even more peaceful than he remembered. The old magic of the property had drawn him out of town today despite warning himself that it might evoke more regrets or make him more dissatisfied with the new existence he had created for himself. Finding George here had been unbelievable but now that he was over the initial shock, Max decided that it was the way it should be. The place had been perfect in his memory and it could never be perfect unless George was here. He could see her now, bent over in the extensive, walled vegetable garden, cutting something leafy and green which she placed in a flat basket beside her. She straightened and moved towards another of the raised beds in the elegantly patterned garden.

It was a work of art, that garden. Narrow paths ran between beds that were triangle-shaped, coming out from a centre circle like the spokes of a wheel. The circular centre contained a bed of what looked like herbs surrounding a scarecrow with a very friendly face. Teepee-like frames of bamboo were regularly spaced and had young pea and bean plants scrambling up the support. The patch of ground had been wasteland bordering the old orchard when he had last been here. Now it looked like it could produce enough fresh food to feed a small army. George bent over again. She was pulling baby carrots from the well-tilled soil.

Max sucked in a deep breath. The cotton knit bike shorts George was wearing fitted very snugly. When he'd gripped her shoulders earlier, he'd had the unsettling impression that George wasn't wearing a bra. He took a moment or two now to try and dampen the desire he had for this woman. Take it slowly, he warned himself. He had to be sure that it was what George wanted as well. God, the sheer luck of finding her here—and living alone.

Max had spent the last week trying to think of some way of being alone with George. He had planned to catch her attention in the emergency department on the first day he was back at work after his days off but there hadn't been a single helicopter mission that day and he had waited patiently in vain. During her days off, Max had even rung the communications centre of the emergency services, hoping to find someone he might have known years ago who would be happy to let him know her new address. But the staff had all changed and personal information hadn't been forthcoming. It was a plot, he had informed Dougal only this morning. He and George were simply not meant to get back together.

Dougal had said nonsense and had told Max to remember now much they had once had. So Max had remembered, off and on, all day and the memories of living here—with George— had been enough to make him borrow Dougal's car as soon as he'd finished work and head out of the city. Just to see if the house was still here. Maybe it would be a symbol for the potential survival of other things as well.

'Hey!' Max was in control enough to move closer to where George was working. 'What's with the hens? Are they on strike?'

George straightened, tossing her head to clear the fall of black hair across her face. 'You weren't looking for eggs in the hen house, were you?'

'Of course.'

George tucked the errant tresses of hair behind her ear. 'They never lay eggs in the hen house.'

'Of course not. How silly of me.' Max tilted his head. 'Why didn't you tell me that before?'

'I forgot.' George looked embarrassed. 'I was thinking about something else.'

'Hmm.' Max decided it would be prudent not to press the matter further. 'Where *do* they lay eggs, then?'

'I'll show you.' George opened a tiny gate. She put her flat basket down on the broad top of the stone wall.

'Did you make the vegetable garden?' Max queried.

George nodded. 'I built the walls to keep the rabbits out. And Jacob,' she added thoughtfully. 'He's rather fond of vegetables.' She told Max about the donkey's recent escapade into the neighbour's garden. They were both laughing as she led the way through the orchard towards another old shed. This one was made of corrugated iron and was higher than the stable block.

'The hay barn,' George reminded Max unnecessarily. Bales of hay were stacked up to the roof around the edges and looked as though they had been there for a very long time. Bales had been removed from the centre area in a haphazard fashion and the strings had rotted on many of those remaining so that the hay had spilled out to dull the sharp edges of the stack.

'I only use this old hay to mulch the garden,' George explained. 'Watch out for soft spots. Not that you'll hurt yourself if you fall.' She scrambled up over several bales, then paused briefly to pick up two large brown eggs. 'See? They'll be all over the place.' She put the eggs down on the edge of a nearby bale. 'I forgot to bring something to carry them in.'

'Here.' Max stripped off his shirt and spread it out on the hay. He put the eggs George had found on top of the shirt. 'It's already dirty,' he told George. 'Carrying a few eggs won't make any difference.'

George wasn't convinced about that. The sight of Max, naked from the waist up, was already making a considerable difference as far as she was concerned. She tried to distract herself by searching for some more eggs. The number found grew rapidly and it became a contest to see who could find the next hidden clutch. It was more fun than any treasure hunt Max could remember. They kept it up until the light was clearly fading. They both had hay all through their hair and the echoes of their laughter still rang within the corrugated iron of the walls.

'We'll have to put these in water to see if any float,' George told Max. 'Some of them must be ancient by now.'

Max slid down from the very top of the stack, coming to a halt close to George who stood in the centre. Max's shirt, now covered with several dozen eggs, lay on a bale to one side at eye level. Max ignored the haul. He reached out and pulled a stalk of hay from George's hair.

'I've missed you,' he said softly. 'A lot more than I realised.'

'I've missed you, too, Max.'

Max smiled rather sadly. 'We made a lot of mistakes, didn't we?'

George simply nodded. Max went to pick out another piece of hay but his hand dropped to stroke George's cheek instead.

'I still feel the same way about you, George.'

George stood very still. Max's hair was full of hay. His jeans were ripped and his bare chest was dusty. A shred of hay lay caught in the sparse curls of his chest hair. Surely it wasn't possible that anyone could look more desirable than this man, at this moment.

'I need you, George.'

'I need you, too, Max.'

Max's hand was threading itself through George's hair. He bent his head closer. He swallowed audibly. 'God,' he breathed. 'I want you.'

Words were almost beyond George. She pressed the palms of her hands against Max's chest, running them lightly up over nipples as hard as pebbles. She pressed closer.

'I want you, too, Max,' she whispered.

With a groan, Max lowered his head to cover her lips with his own. It was just like the first kiss they'd ever had. A tentative exploration of each other's taste and touch. And it was nothing like the first kiss they'd ever had because they remembered so quickly exactly what it was like and where it would lead.

Max's lips moved to George's throat and she tilted her head back with a sigh. His fingers reached for the first button of her shirt and then the second. George was pressed back against the prickly wall of hay and almost welcomed the distraction of the discomfort. It was too much. *Max* was too much. She ran her fingers through the thick waves of his dark hair and groaned as Max slid his hand inside her shirt. He drew her closer, his other hand cupping her bottom. His fingers moved and tightened.

'Good lord, George,' Max raised his head. 'You're not wearing a bra *or* knickers!'

'I got dressed in a hurry.' George's hand had found the tear in Max's jeans. She wondered if the feel of those silky black briefs would be as tantalising as the sight of them had been.

'I wouldn't do that if I were you.' Max had her pinned to the hay bales now, one hand on either side of her head, the length of his body covering hers. 'Not if you have any intention of this not going any further.'

George slid her hand inside the tear by way of an answer. Max caught his breath. 'I haven't got anything with me,' he said a little hoarsely. 'Condoms, I mean.'

'It's OK,' George said quickly. She didn't want to discuss safe sex or birth control. Especially birth control.

But Max did. 'What do you mean, George? Are you on the Pill?' He drew back far enough to see her face clearly. 'You said you weren't in a relationship. That you were single.'

'I am.' George licked suddenly dry lips. 'I'm not on the Pill.'

'So what are you using? A diaphragm? An IUD?'

'No.'

'Are you using anything?'

'No.' George's responses were getting quieter.

Max frowned. 'You mean the possibility of an accidental pregnancy doesn't bother you?'

'It's highly unlikely—especially at my age,' George said lightly. 'And even if it *did* happen, it wouldn't be a total disaster.'

'What?' Max straightened, backing further away from George.

'I mean that I wouldn't be devastated if I did get p—pregnant.' George stammered slightly over the last word. Somehow, hearing the words made it all seem very different to the fantasies she had been building about holding Max's baby.

'My God!' Max stepped back putting a clear distance between himself and George. 'Maybe Dougal *was* right. The alarm's gone off.'

'What?' George was aware of the gaping front of her shirt. She pulled the edges together. 'What are you talking about, Max?'

'Your biological clock. The one you hit the snooze button on five years ago. Remember?' Max sounded angry now. 'It's not me you want, is it, George? You want a *baby*.'

The guilty flush on her face, clearly visible even in the twilight, said it all. And yet it didn't say nearly enough. How could she tell Max that it was him she wanted? She wanted him so much that if she couldn't have him she'd settle for just a part of him. She couldn't tell him because there was an element of truth in his accusation. She *did* want a baby. She needed to refocus her life. There was far too much to try and explain, and if Max was as angry as he looked right now then he wouldn't be willing to listen. George still had to try.

'It's *you* I want, Max. I always have. There's never been anyone else.'

'Sure.' Max wasn't looking at George. His gaze scanned the hay bales around them. 'There's probably no one else who could conveniently pop in for a few weeks and then disappear again to the other side of the world.' He spotted his shirt and took two strides towards it. 'What is it this time, George? Have you decided to prove to the world that you can do it all by yourself? Are you going to combine single parenthood and a full-time career now?'

Max jerked his shirt roughly from beneath the eggs. Several rolled and bounced off the edge of the hay bale, breaking into puddles. 'Sorry, George, but you can count me out.' Max pulled the shirt over his head. 'There's no way I'm going to risk fathering a child that I'm not going to watch grow up. You're just using me, George. I can't believe that even you could be so selfish.'

Max crouched, using one hand as a pivot to jump to the ground. He strode off, without a backward glance, and was out of sight almost instantly. George stood still for a moment longer. Why hadn't she simply lied and said she was on the Pill? The answer to that was easy. She couldn't have told a lie—not just because Max might have assumed she'd been lying when she'd said there was no one else in her life. She had never lied to Max and certainly wasn't about to start now.

George sighed miserably. No wonder he was so angry. The desire to get pregnant did sound calculating—out of context with the rest of her life and divorced from her feelings about Max. It also sounded selfish. The plan was only perfect from her own point of view. She hadn't really thought about it from Max's perspective. Or the baby's. But 'even you'? Had she left such a lasting impression of being self-centred on Max when she had stood her ground, wanting to follow her own career opportunities?

Maybe she had. George watched as the contents of the eggs soaked into the hay, leaving shells as broken as her recent dreams.

Maybe she had.

CHAPTER SEVEN

'YOU'RE a bastard, Max.'

'Sorry?' Max looked up from his paperwork with a startled expression.

Dougal Donaldson hopped a step closer to the desk, leaning comfortably on his underarm crutches. 'I've been thinking all morning about what you told me when you came home last night and when I came to my inevitable conclusion, I just had to come and tell you.'

'Tell me what?' Max had a thundering headache which he was blaming on the heavy workload in the emergency department. He was sure he hadn't downed that much bourbon when relating the cause of his disturbed mood to the receptive audience Dougal had provided the previous evening.

'That you're a bastard,' Dougal repeated obligingly.

'Thanks, mate.' Max signed the laboratory request forms, put them inside the bag with the blood samples and strode down the corridor to despatch the parcel via the vacuum system.

Annoyingly, Dougal kept pace with him quite easily. His friend was getting far too mobile on those crutches. 'You've burned your bridges now,' Dougal continued relentlessly. 'Cooked your goose, mate—and it was all there for you. On a plate by the sound of things.'

Max snorted derisively, casting a quick glance around the corridor. A consultant went past into the relatives' room. No one was within earshot. 'Are you suggesting I should have gone along with it? She was just using me as a potential father for her child. Have you any idea how humiliating it was, being told that I would fill the bill?'

'Did she *say* that, precisely?'

'She didn't need to. She had no intention of bothering with birth control. You were right. The alarm's gone off. She wants a baby.'

'So? You want kids, don't you?'

'Of course I do. But I want to be around while they grow up, thank you very much. I want them to have a whole family—preferably with siblings and a mother who's around if they need a plaster stuck on their knees.'

'And who would you want to be their mother?'

'That's got nothing to do with it.'

'It's got everything to do with it.' Dougal hopped closer to the wall as a stretcher was pushed between the two men. Then he moved back to corner Max again. 'Who would it be?' he persisted.

'You know the answer to that.'

Dougal nodded. 'And I know why, mate. Because you don't want anyone else. You love the woman.' He sighed as though the point he was making should be obvious. 'Why do think that George picked you?'

'Takes two to make a baby,' Max muttered. 'Maybe I was just available—and more than willing.'

'You think you're the only one who'd be willing?' Dougal shook his head. 'Use your brains, man. George could take her pick. Hell, I'd probably fight to get further up the queue myself but I wouldn't stand a chance.'

'No.' Max grinned half-heartedly. 'I'd probably flatten you myself.'

'Maybe George does want a baby,' Dougal said slowly. 'But maybe that's secondary to wanting its father. Have you thought of that?'

Max grunted noncommittally. He *had* thought of that. He'd decided he'd been too harsh with George well before Dougal had arrived to interrupt his working day. He had been dealing with similar interruptions to his own thoughts for more than twelve hours now. Sleep had proved impossible and the fragments of time between patients this morning had provided plenty more opportunities for snippets of the confrontation in the hay barn to keep resurrecting themselves. Things that George had said, especially the claim that it was him she wanted and always had. That there had never been anyone else.

Max sighed. 'I've got work to do, Dougal. I've been flat out since I came on duty at 7 a.m. It's now 1 p.m. and I haven't even had a morning teabreak yet. Is there any other reason for you being here other than to let me know what a bastard I am?'

'I'm bored at home,' Dougal complained. 'I thought I might hang around and watch the action here. I might learn something interesting.'

'You might get in the way,' Max observed. He watched Dougal manoeuvre himself to make enough space for a bed to be wheeled past. A nurse excused herself and reached past Max to post some blood samples. Max kept moving, having cleared the way for her. He had a post-ictal patient he needed to check in Cubicle 3 and a hyoptensive man in Resus 4 that looked like he might be going into heart failure.

'All right. I suppose I'd better go home,' Dougal conceded. 'I've already learned something interesting anyway.'

'Oh?'

'They're about to advertise for a full-time doctor out at the rescue helicopter base. I thought I might try and extend my working visa and apply for it. Be fun for a while.'

'Fun?'

'Exciting!' Dougal's face shone with enthusiasm. 'Real front-line emergency work. Imagine the sort of conditions you'd have to work under. The challenges you'd get. I wouldn't want to do it for ever but it would be a fantastic experience.' He grinned at Max. 'I think I'll go and do some research this afternoon. I'll see what information I can dig up at the library about the service.'

'What would they know about it?'

'They keep copies of the local newspaper on computer record. The articles are a fount of information,' Dougal claimed. 'They always write up the major cases and it would give a good indication of the sort of work a doctor would be expected to deal with.'

Max pulled back the curtain to Resus 4. 'Have a good time,' he said wearily. 'Who's cooking tonight?'

'You are.' Dougal's smile was wicked. 'And make it meat loaf. I'm still hanging out to try the stuff.'

The excitement of doing front-line emergency work under difficult and often dangerous conditions seemed like a distant memory. Five years ago this would have been just the sort of mission George had desperately hoped to be sent on. A fisherman on a boat several miles offshore had been caught in the machinery used to bring the giant nets on board. His arm had been partially severed and he'd lost a great deal of blood. The man was now semi-conscious. At least a Status 2 patient. Possibly Status 1 if the blood loss had been severe enough. He lay on the bow deck of a small commercial trawler which was rolling in a heavy sea. The master of the boat had been instructed via radio to turn downwind and keep enough speed on the vessel to control the steering.

Ted Scott, the helicopter pilot, was in constant contact with the boat's skipper. The rescue crew had all breathed a sigh of relief on finding that the boat's crew was English-speaking. The operation was dangerous enough without having to worry about instructions being misinterpreted. Communication with the boat was not allowed to interfere with the standard voice procedures between the helicopter crew members.

'Turning base leg.'

'Roger.' Murray was the winch operator again today.

'Clear to open door.'

'Door back and locked.' Murray brought the hook inboard but not to attach to George's harness. This time he attached the end of a coiled rope with a weighted end.

'Deploying Hi Line.' Murray started feeding out the weighted end of the rope towards the deck of the vessel.

'Roger.' Ted made sure the skipper was listening. 'Do not secure the line to any part of the vessel,' Ted reminded him. 'I repeat—do *not* attach the line.'

'Roger.' The skipper sounded calm. 'We're ready for you.'

'Hi Line deployed.' Murray was watching for the crew on board the boat to catch the line. He had to be sure it didn't tangle in any of the rigging above deck. 'Has Hi Line,' he informed Ted. 'Back and right to your target.' Murray kept feeding out slack while Ted manoeuvred to get a hover reference. He connected the Hi Line quick release hook to the extension line and then to the hoist hook.

George was ready for her part of the procedure. She attached herself to the winch hook and removed her seat belt. 'Moving George to door,' Murray relayed to Ted. 'Clear skids.'

'Clear skids.'

With the signal of Murray's tap on her shoulder, George stood up on the skids.

'Clear to boom out.'

'Clear.'

George felt her weight taken up by the winch. Murray then attached a stretcher and trauma pack to the short extension on the winch hook. From a safety point of view it would have been preferable to winch the injured man with a nappy harness—the less time spent over the boat the better—but the patient's condition was too serious to allow the option. George steadied the lightweight stretcher dangling between her legs as she was winched down towards the boat.

'Minus fifteen,' she warned Murray. 'Minus ten.' The descent slowed. George could see the boat to her right side. She was now below the level of the masts and aerials which looked alarmingly close.

'Pull the line aboard,' Ted instructed the skipper.

Two crewmen on board the boat were pulling on the weighted rope. George swung slowly sideways as she descended the last few feet and pulled the stretcher up to clear her knees. The pitch of the boat made George's feet contact the deck with a jarring thud that sent a shaft of pain through her lower back. George knew, at that point, that this could well be the last winching operation she would ever do, but the acceptance of that knowledge would only come later. She couldn't afford to think about herself right now.

The fluid replacement and oxygen therapy badly needed by the shocked victim would have to wait until they were on board the helicopter. All George did on deck was to remove the inadequate tourniquet the ship's first-aid officer had applied, replacing it with a pressure bandage that would control any further blood loss. Secured onto the stretcher, George got several crewmen to help lift and hold her patient on the deck's railing. The Hi Line was deployed again, used to bring the winch hook across to the boat. Balancing on the railing, George attached the hook to the stretcher's lifting harness first, then attached herself, with the trauma pack also secured from her own harness.

'Weight's coming on.' Murray responded to George's thumbs-up signal. 'You have the weight,' he informed Ted.

The extra line was fed out with enough tension to reduce swing until the load was clear of the boat and its rigging.

'Clear to winch,' Murray requested.

Ted had relocated his hover reference. 'Clear,' he responded.

'Twenty feet, Fifteen...' The procedure seemed to George to be taking a long time. 'Ten...nine...eight...stretcher just below skids,' Murray told Ted. 'Stretcher at door. Booming in.'

George hooked onto an anchor strap and released herself from the winch cable. She helped manoeuvre the stretcher head first into the helicopter before following it in.

'Winch complete. Ready for Hi Line retrieval,' Murray continued. He coiled the rope loosely on the floor as he pulled it in by hand. The side door was closed. 'Secure aft,' Murray reported. 'Clear to move away.'

The next hour passed in something of a blur for George. The fisherman needed aggressive treatment to deal with the state of hypovolaemic shock he was in. George and Murray inserted two wide-bore IV lines and ran in fluids as quickly as possible to try and bring his systolic blood pressure up to 90 millimetres mercury. They maintained an open airway by use of a nasopharyngeal tube and assisted his breathing with positive pressure ventilation and supplemental oxygen. They kept his feet elevated and monitored his body temperature along with other vital signs.

The resuscitation team waiting at the hospital took over the care of the man immediately but both George and Murray stayed with their patient, observing the continuation of their treatment until the man's condition was stable enough for him to be taken to Theatre. He would probably lose his left arm from below the elbow but at least it now seemed likely that he would survive.

'We've got the full write-up of this mission to do,' Murray told George wearily. 'We'd better get on with it or we won't have a hope of getting home on time.'

George nodded. She wanted to get home rather badly. She was exhausted, her back hurt and she would rather not be anywhere near John Maxwell at this moment. It had been easy enough to avoid any eye contact while the emergency had been dealt with and the doctor's attention firmly on his patient, but now Max was writing up his own paperwork on the other side of the desk Murray had chosen to dump their forms and notes on.

Murray was eyeing George. 'Are you OK?'

'Fine,' George said shortly. She had caught the quick transfer of Max's gaze towards herself. 'I'm just hot. I'm cooking in this immersion suit.'

'Take it off,' Murray suggested.

'No, thanks.' George had only her underwear on beneath the wetsuit-type garment.

Murray grinned. 'I think there's a spare flight suit around. I'll see if I can track it down.'

Before George had a chance to protest, Murray was gone, leaving her virtually alone with Max. Other staff continued their duties around the desk but it felt like an island with no chance of a quick rescue. George sat down gingerly and picked up a pen. At least she could make a start on the incident report. George was aware that Max was doing the opposite. He had put down his pen and abandoned his own paperwork.

'You don't look very comfortable,' he commented.

'Hardly surprising.' George didn't look up. 'I can find somewhere else to work, if you prefer.'

'No.' Max's response was quick. 'Please, don't. I owe you an apology.'

George was silent. The patient details she needed to fill in were a meaningless jumble of letters in front of her.

'I overreacted last night,' Max said quietly. 'I'm sorry, George.'

'Forget it,' George said tightly. 'You were right. I was being irresponsible and selfish.' She raised her gaze for only a second. 'But I guess that's nothing new, is it?' The blame George had heaped on herself in the wake of last night's disastrous encounter in the hay barn had left her feeling completely at fault. She had stripped her self-esteem to an all-time low. Murray reappeared before Max had time to respond.

'Here you go,' he told George. 'I think it belongs to Ross but he won't mind. You'll have to roll the legs and sleeves up a fair bit, though.'

'Thanks.' George took the rolled-up pair of orange overalls. 'I'll go and change.' She eased herself to her feet carefully but was unable to completely conceal the discomfort the movement caused.

Murray frowned. 'You came down on deck with a hell of a bump,' he reminded George. 'Do you need to get your back checked out?'

'No.' George glared at Murray, warning him not to pursue the matter.

Max focused on Murray. 'What do you mean, ''a hell of a bump''?' he queried tersely.

'It's inevitable with a boat winch on heavy seas,' Murray told him. 'You can winch in with all the care in the world but one second the deck's way below and the next it's coming up to meet you with a crunch. Even when the boat crew knows what it's doing with the Hi Line, it's tricky.'

'What's a Hi Line?'

George left Murray explaining the technicalities of a boat winching mission to Max. They were still discussing the subject when she returned, having changed into the cooler uniform and discreetly swallowed a couple of Panadol tablets to deal with her back pain.

Already feeling a lot better, George smiled at her partner.

'Finished the paperwork, then, Mozzie?'

'Haven't started,' Murray confessed. 'Blame Max here. He seems to have developed a keen interest in helicopter work.'

'You do an amazing job.' Max was looking directly at George now. 'That chap would have died if you hadn't got him off the boat and got treatment under way as quickly as you did. I'm impressed.'

'Thanks.' George tried to sound offhand but the eye contact caught her. Max was genuinely impressed and the respect for what she did was something new. It was a bit late coming but surprisingly welcome nonetheless. 'You did OK, too,' she said lightly. 'Not much point retrieving patients if they don't get the care they need at this end.'

'We're all part of the same team,' Murray put in. He paused in his rapid scribbling to give George a curious glance. Then he raised an eyebrow in Max's direction. 'You should come out to the base one day and see what it's all about. Did you know they've decided to employ a doctor full time out there?'

'I heard.' Max nodded. 'And I might take you up on that offer, Murray. I wouldn't mind knowing a bit more about the helicopter rescue service.'

George swallowed hard. 'I'll collect the stretcher and clean up our gear,' she excused herself. 'I'll be up on the roof when you've finished, Mozzie.' She frowned. 'I think I'll take Ted a cup of tea and an aspirin or two. He hasn't been looking that well all day.'

'He's coming down with a cold or flu or something. Aspirin sounds like a good idea. I won't be long here,' Murray assured her, 'then Ted can get home for some TLC.'

George turned away from the men, unsuccessfully trying to concentrate on Ted and how he might be feeling. She made tea in a polystyrene cup and raided the drugs cupboard for some aspirin. Having arrived on the rooftop again, George left Ted gratefully sipping his drink to pace the perimeter of the hospital roof. She gazed down at the river, the manicured green spaces and the canopy of all the lovely old trees in the botanical gardens without her usual appreciation of the scene's beauty.

Why would Max pick now to express an interest in her job? To let her know that he admired the career she had chosen. The end of her ability to perform was in sight. If she stayed in the ambulance service at all she was going to be confined to a desk job that was unlikely to impress anyone. It was too late for Max to learn to appreciate the pull of her career. And it was too late for her to dampen the wild desire to replace her career with a family. The desire which had led to Max making assumptions that would be virtually impossible to change. The damage had been done and she had no one to blame but herself.

The loaf-shaped offering of baked, minced beef, onions and seasoning looked unappetising. When Max carved off a slice, the loaf crumbled and the serving looked even worse by the time he had transferred it to a plate.

'That,' he informed Dougal, 'is meat loaf.'

'Looks like haggis,' Dougal said cheerfully. 'I think I'm going to like it.' He picked up his fork.

'It might need some tomato sauce.' Max suggested. Dougal had stopped chewing and was eyeing him thoughtfully.

'No, it's great. I love it. Could do with a beer to wash it down, though.'

'Good idea.' Max returned to the table, having collected some icy bottles of lager from the fridge. He flipped the top off one and took a long swallow. Dougal was watching him again. Max raised his eyebrows. 'Have I sprouted an extra ear or are you just overcome with awe at my ability to cook appallingly bad food?'

Dougal grinned. He pushed his plate to one side and picked up his beer. 'We could always order in a pizza.'

'Yeah.' Max ignored his own plate. He wasn't particularly hungry anyway. 'So, what's on your mind, then?'

'Helicopters,' Dougal responded promptly.

'Did you find out anything?'

'More than I expected, in fact. The system for searching newspaper articles is all computerised. Type in a key word and—bingo—umpteen articles to check out.'

'And?' Max could see that Dougal was keen to share something.

'It's an amazing job, Max. They get sent to every major disaster for hundreds of miles.

Train and car smashes, building and bridge collapses, farm and mountaineering accidents, avalanches—you name it, they're there.' Dougal shook his head in awe. 'They rescue people off mountains, farms, motorways— even boats!'

Max nodded. 'They had a mission at sea this afternoon. George winched in to get a chap who tried to pull his arm off in some machinery. They did a great job, too. Had him virtually stabilised by the time they got to the hospital.'

'She's an amazing woman. Quite phenomenal, in fact.'

'Don't start that again,' Max groaned. 'I thought you'd agreed she wasn't the one for you.'

'This has nothing to do with what I think of George,' Dougal said slowly. 'I found something that maybe you should read yourself.' He reached for a manila folder, left on the table beside the propped-up crutches. Leafing through printouts of newspaper articles, Dougal selected one and handed it to Max.

The figure waving from the interior of the helicopter cockpit was instantly recognisable.

George looked very pleased with herself. As Max's eye caught the headline, he realised why. 'Amazing Recovery By Paramedic', he read. Horrified, Max scanned the smaller print rapidly. ''After near tragedy when a training exercise turned to disaster, Georgina Collins has astounded her doctors and colleagues by making a full recovery and returning to work full time as a helicopter rescue paramedic.''

Max held his breath as he read the account of the winching accident, six months prior to the article being written, that had left George lying on a mountainside with a fractured spine. He shook his head at the rescue mission that had been undertaken to retrieve her and the summary of her stay in the spinal injuries unit. Finally, more carefully, he read of her successful return to full mobility. 'My job is my life. I couldn't imagine doing anything else,' George was quoted as saying. Max checked the date. Two and a half years ago.

Dougal waited in silence until Max finally looked up.

'She could have been killed,' Max said quietly.

'Almost was, by the sound of it,' Dougal
agreed. 'Hasn't stopped her, though, has it?'

'It's a bloody dangerous job.'

'It's put me off.' Dougal took a long swallow from his bottle of lager. 'I won't be applying for that position at the base.'

'No? Good.' Max was still staring at the
photograph accompanying the article. 'Because I think I might.'

'Might what?'

'Apply for the position.'

'Are you crazy?' Dougal's jaw dropped noticeably. 'What about your job at the Royal?'

'I'm not leaving this country without
George,' Max informed his friend. 'I might not
want to leave at all. And I need a bit more
time to sort things out.'

'So keep your feet on the ground. We're
short of consultants in the emergency department. They'll be advertising a position soon.'

'I'll see a lot more of George if I'm on the
base.'

'You'll be putting yourself at considerable
physical risk, mate.'

'You said yourself, only this afternoon, what
exciting potential the job had.'

'That was before I read about this.' Dougal waved at the article.

'And how often does this sort of incident happen? Did you read about any more?'

'No.'

'And it wasn't enough to put George off, was it?'

'No,' Dougal repeated obligingly.

'Well, you know what they say, mate.'

'What's that?'

Max smiled slowly. 'If you can't beat them—join them.'

CHAPTER EIGHT

'RED'S a bit keen this morning, isn't he?'

'How's that?' Murray Peters waited for George to extract her lunch-box from the back of her car and lock up.

'It's not even 7 a.m. and the chopper's out, ready to go. We haven't got some early mission lined up that nobody told me about, have we?'

Murray shook his head. 'Not that I've heard. Anyway, it's not Ted. He's got blocked ears with that cold he was coming down with yesterday. He could clear them with medication but it's better if he doesn't fly today. Ripper's filling in for him.'

'Oh.' George digested the news with some dismay. 'That explains the enthusiasm, then. Ted would at least have had a coffee before starting the day.'

'We're going to have one,' Murray assured George. 'I haven't told you what we have to get stuck into this morning if we don't get a job.'

George groaned. 'Not the stocktaking.' The large supply room hadn't been properly tidied or checked for some time. It was going to be a long and boring task to find and reorder everything that wasn't up to minimum numbers. The prospect of an enjoyable day at work took a second knock and George hadn't even stepped into the hangar yet.

Murray nodded. ''Fraid so. And what's more, Phil Warrington's planning a visit some time this morning. Not only will we have to be seen to be doing the stocktake, my guess is that he wants to talk to you about that job in town.'

'I should have followed Ted's example and stayed home,' George sighed. 'How do you know about all this?'

'I had a long chat to Stretch last night. He and Ross are coming in today as well. Apparently they've found all that gear that got washed off the yacht on the job they had the other day. It's got to be sorted and cleaned.'

'Going to be a fun day all round,' George muttered. She returned the wave that came from the helicopter cockpit. Jack Burgess was making sure he would be ready to take off at a moment's notice. 'For once I won't complain if we don't get any calls,' George said wearily. 'I hope it's dead quiet like that day we had last week.'

'We'd better get something.' Murray grinned. 'John Maxwell rang me last night as well. He's got a day off and wants to come for a visit. Wouldn't want him to think the job's totally lacking in any excitement.'

Even the prospect of seeing Max didn't raise George's negative anticipation of the day ahead. Max might have apologised for his storming off the night before last. He might have expressed admiration for the job she'd done yesterday, but his approaches couldn't erase the grievances they had accumulated between them. And it couldn't lessen the crushing disappointment that George's failure to make a fresh start with Max had engendered. Not that George was going to let such a personal attitude affect her work. After an excellent cup of coffee, she smiled brightly at Murray.

'Let's get stuck in, then,' she suggested, 'and get this stocktaking out of the way.'

By 8.30 a.m. there had been no calls for a helicopter rescue. George and Murray were well into their sorting and recording of supplies.

'Let's do the oxygen masks,' Murray decided. 'How many adult acutes should we have on hand?'

George checked the sheet. 'Fifty.'

'We're down to ten. What about nebulisers?'

'Twenty.' George was writing down the shortfall in acute masks. They finished the mask tally quickly and moved on to the stack of cervical collars.

'We're missing a ''no neck'' and need two more ''regulars'',' Murray stated. He paused and glanced at George as she finished writing. 'What are you going to say to Phil about the job?'

'I don't know.' George looked up from her clipboard and sighed. 'It's not an easy decision.'

'I know.' Murray looked sympathetic.

'When I first came out here, I wanted this job more than anything I'd ever wanted in my life. Do you know, I even broke off my engagement because I couldn't bear to leave town and lose the opportunity to work here?'

'I never knew that!' Murray looked shocked now.

'He'd left before I started here,' George explained. 'There didn't seem any point talking about it. Even a lot of the road crews never knew. We didn't have that much time together so we tended to stay home and not socialise much. M—' George just stopped herself before revealing Max's name. 'My fiancé's work hours were even worse than mine at times.'

'What did he do?' Murray poked at a box of crêpe bandages, counting the plastic wrapped rolls.

'He was a doctor.'

'We've got twenty-five three-inch bandages and nineteen four-inch.'

'That'll do for the moment.' George ticked off the sections on her check sheet.

Murray peered into a box of gauze dressings. 'So, this doctor. Anyone I know?'

'Not really.' George kept her gaze on the clipboard. It wasn't a lie. After all, Murray had only had his first real conversation with Max the day before. 'There should be ten large dressings.'

'Down to three,' Murray reported. He eyed George curiously. 'And there's never been anyone else?'

'Nothing that went anywhere at all,' George stated flatly. 'I don't think there ever could be.'

Murray's eyes crinkled with the appearance of concerned lines that George knew very well. Murray Peters was a kind man and a good friend. His advice about her career direction, or anything else for that matter, would be worth listening to.

'Does he regret the break-up as much as you do?'

George thought back to the encounter in the hay barn. He had missed her, he'd said. He needed her. He wanted her. 'I think…' George felt her cheeks colouring. 'I think that's possible.'

'Did he get married?'

'No.'

'Do you still see him?'

'A bit. But only recently.' George wanted to change the subject. Max could arrive at the base at any minute. She didn't want Murray saying anything—however well intentioned—that might make things more difficult. 'How are we off for medium-sized dressings, then?'

Murray ignored the query. 'Life's a funny thing,' he said casually. 'Sometimes you get to a crossroads and you think you take the right path but then you find out a bit further down the track that maybe it wasn't.' He raised his eyebrows encouragingly. 'You can always duck off the path you chose and make a new track to try and join up to the other one again. Everybody has to do it at times. You just hope that you notice the wrong direction before it goes too far and gets into really rough country.'

George liked the analogy. 'There might be a jungle between my paths by now. With a river full of man-eating crocodiles.'

'So?' Murray grinned. 'Build a bridge.'

George laughed. 'You make it sound so easy.'

'No.' Murray sobered quickly. 'The most worthwhile things in life are never easy.'

'No,' George agreed. The conversation was in danger of becoming too heavy. Imagine if she burst into tears and started to tell Murray the whole sorry story? 'Like this stocktake,' she added lightly. 'Come on, I can see light at the end of the tunnel now. How many medium dressings have we got?'

By lunchtime, the stocktake was complete, Phil Warrington had been and gone, having had a long talk to George, and there had still been no calls for a helicopter. Mike Bingham and Ross White had arrived with a carload of gear that had been trawled out of the sea and delivered to the central police station yesterday. Not looking forward to spending part of their day off attending to the clean-up required, the two men went off to the staffroom to fortify themselves with coffee first. Max had also arrived and was being given some guidelines on safety around helicopters by Murray and Jack.

'You've got to stay in my line of vision at all times,' Jack directed. 'Never approach a helicopter from the rear.'

'Never approach or leave a helicopter when the engine and rotors are running down or starting up,' Murray added.

'And if you get blinded by dust or grit from the rotor wash while it's hovering and you're getting on or off, then crouch lower or sit down and wait for help.'

'OK.' Max was soaking in all the instructions.

'I'll see if I can find a spare flight suit to fit you.' Murray eyed Max's tall and broad-shouldered figure. 'You'll need a helmet as well.'

'Are you expecting a mission?'

'No.' It was George who spoke. 'It's been dead quiet all morning. Might stay that way all day.' Her pager sounded as she spoke. So did Murray's. Jack's cellphone began ringing.

'*Yes!*' Jack was grinning broadly. 'Thanks, George. You've broken the drought.'

Suddenly, it was all go. The job was urgent. A man had been found on a riverbank, pinned under a farm bike which had rolled. A road crew had been despatched but the target area was isolated and the helicopter would be much faster. The patient was only semi-conscious and could well be seriously injured.

It was George who quickly found Max the overalls and helmet. Murray was already on board the helicopter as Jack warmed up the engine. He was using the radio, getting more information and relaying instructions to the people on the scene. The victim was breathing well enough at the moment and had been trapped for some time so instructions were given not to lift the roll bar of the bike which was pinning the man to the ground. Internal injuries from a crushing force always had to be suspected and it could cause serious internal bleeding. The object causing the crush injury, in this case the roll bar of the bike, could also be applying enough pressure to be controlling the bleeding and a victim could deteriorate rapidly when the pressure was lifted.

Murray wanted to be there when the bar was removed and have IV fluids already run in to start counteracting the state of shock that could well be a result of the manoeuvre. The timing of the accident wasn't known precisely but the farm worker had been missing for hours. A few more minutes wouldn't make much difference.

It was a quick flight over flat land. Jack couldn't show off his flying skills to Max who sat up front beside the young pilot. Even following the river towards the gorge, Jack refrained from the twists and turns he would normally have indulged in. There was no question of difficult access or a need for winching. The shingle shoreline of the river was quite wide enough for landing and track marks from vehicles who used the area to launch boats could be seen, which indicated that the shingle was firm enough for safety.

The shingle was softer towards the bank. The farm bike had rolled from an area several metres up where the ground was flat enough for fence posts to be driven in. The broken fencing that had attracted the attention of the farmhand was clearly visible—a fencepost dangling free like a broken tooth, creating a hole easily big enough for sheep to use as an escape route. The bike now lay upside down at the base of the bank. The figure of the trapped victim lay partially obscured by both the vehicle and the shingle. Several people now stood nearby. One man was crouching beside the victim's head. He looked enormously relieved at the sight of the approaching rescue crew.

'Told you they'd be here soon, Aaron. We'll have you out in no time.'

'Hi, Aaron.' George wanted to assess the young man's level of consciousness. 'I'm George and this is Murray and Max. How's it going?'

The response was a moan, followed by speech that was largely incomprehensible. Aaron's eyes closed again. The effort to communicate stopped.

'Has he been talking to you?' Max asked his companion.

'Up until a minute or two ago.'

'What did he say about his injuries?' Murray was kneeling, a hand thrust behind the roll bar of the bike resting on Aaron's abdomen as he assessed respiration rate and depth. George was feeling the pulse at his neck, having applied an oxygen mask and turned on the flow.

'Tachycardia,' she reported. 'One-forty. A few VPBs as well.'

'Respiration rate of 30—and shallow,' Murray added.

'He said he couldn't feel or move his legs at all and it hurt to move his arm. Said he couldn't breathe properly and kept asking us to get the bar off him, but we were told to wait for you guys.'

'Any idea how long he's been trapped?'

'Could have been hours. He went out at 6.30 a.m. but we don't know whether checking the fence was the first job he did.'

'We need a backboard and a collar.' Murray stood up. A spinal injury was high on the list for suspected trauma, given the mechanism of injury and the symptoms Aaron had complained of earlier.

'Let's get an IV in.' Max opened the trauma pack. He eyed the zipped-up compartments. 'Where do I find the cannulae?'

'Here.' George tapped a pocket. 'Wipes and plugs are in here...' She indicated another section. 'Fluid and giving sets are in the bottom. Do you want some help?'

'Get a blood pressure first, would you, please, George? And I'd like a monitor on as well.'

George edged between the two front wheels of the bike and the grassy bank to reach Aaron's other arm. She wrapped the blood-pressure cuff around his upper arm, felt for a radial and then brachial pulse. She placed the disc of the stethoscope at elbow level. 'BP is 85 on 70,' she told Max quickly. 'No radial pulse palpable.'

Max nodded, intent on his own task of inserting the wide-bore cannula into a vein on Aaron's forearm. Murray arrived back, depositing the backboard and extra equipment onto the shingle.

'He's hypotensive,' Max informed Murray. 'Narrow pulse pressure. Can you get the IV running? I want to have a look at his neck veins and trachea alignment before we get a collar on.'

'Trachea's midline,' George said. She had checked when taking Aaron's initial heart rate. 'Veins weren't flat but not distended either.' She was placing ECG electrodes. 'Skin's clammy and cool.'

The young man was in shock. They could anticipate severe abdominal injuries and bleeding from the mechanism of injury but hypovolaemic shock would result in flat neck veins. She could see Max's hand on their patient's neck as she attached the last electrode. She could also see the rope of distended vein as he pulled his hand away. Max caught her eye and she nodded. The sign indicated cardiogenic rather than hypovolaemic shock. George turned on the life pack as she quickly considered the possibilities.

Aaron could have a tension pneumothorax from rib injuries caused by the crush injury from the bar. He could have a tamponade caused by bleeding around his heart. It reminded George of the first patient she had ever worked on with Max. Maybe the crushing force had bruised the heart muscle itself, which could present like an infarct. That would explain the disturbances in rhythm that were showing up now. Maybe, despite his young age, Aaron had had a heart attack and that had been the cause of the accident. Max's thoughts were obviously going through a similar rapid sequence.

'Did Aaron say how the accident happened?' he asked the man who had been beside Aaron when they'd arrived. 'He didn't lose consciousness or suffer chest pain or anything?'

The man shook his head. 'Said the bank caved in. See—you can see the slip. Ground's been wet. That's why we've been having trouble with the fenceposts and the stock getting out.'

Murray gave the bag of IV fluid to Aaron's companion to hold. 'Ready for a collar?' he asked Max.

Max nodded. 'Let's get this bar off his chest.' He looked around. 'We've got plenty of help to lift the bike.'

The men had no trouble lifting the machine clear. They were also keen to co-operate in keeping Aaron's spinal alignment secure as they moved him onto the backboard. It had taken only a few minutes to assess and extricate their patient but it was long enough for Aaron's level of consciousness to slip further and for his condition to deteriorate markedly.

Drugs were drawn up and administered to deal with the now serious disturbances to his heart rhythm. George switched the oxygen mask to a bag-valve mask and assisted Aaron's breathing. About to query the need to intubate their patient, she was diverted by Murray's calm warning that the rhythm had deteriorated further.

'Ventricular fibrillation,' he stated.

The remains of Aaron's shirt were ripped clear. It was Max who slapped the defibrillator pads into place and picked up the paddles.

'Stand clear,' he warned. George lifted the mask away from Aaron's face and wriggled back. 'Are you clear?' Max queried.

'Clear.' George and Murray spoke together.

The single charge was enough to regain a normal rhythm but the extra VPBs returned quickly. George carried on with ventilations. Max was listening to Aaron's chest with a stethoscope.

'Breath sounds are equal. It's not a tension pneumothorax.'

'Heart sounds?' Murray asked.

'Muffled.'

'This bag's nearly empty.' Aaron's friend sounded worried. 'What should I do?'

'I'll get it.' Murray reached for another bag of fluid. He glanced at Max as he did so. 'Beck's triad?' he queried, referring to the three symptoms of low blood pressure, distended neck veins and muffled heart sounds. 'Cardiac tamponade?'

'I reckon. Got the gear for pericardiocentesis?'

'It's not something we're authorised to do,' George told Max. Taking blood from within the pericardial sac was a specialised and invasive procedure that was unlikely to be a priority in the field. The risk of actually puncturing the heart while removing a build-up of blood through a needle would be much higher under the conditions they had of reduced equipment and monitoring facilities available.

'I'm happy to do it,' Max offered. 'I'll need a 20-ml syringe, a long 18-gauge needle, a clamp and some wipes.'

George caught Mozzie's eye. Untreated, a cardiac tamponade would prove rapidly fatal. Aaron had arrested once already and was showing signs of doing so again with the disturbances to his rhythm becoming more prominent. Even the removal of as little as 20 ml of blood from the pericardium could produce an immediate improvement and buy them enough time to get Aaron into hospital.

'I'll get them.' George handed the bag mask to Murray. 'We haven't got any cardiac needles,' she told Max. 'What about the cannula we use for chest decompression?'

'Let's have it.' Max was swabbing a central area on Aaron's chest with alcohol wipes. He held the needle George handed him at right angles to the chest, introduced it and then angled it up towards the left shoulder.

'Keep an eye on the ECG for me,' he warned George. 'Have you got a clamp?'

George had taken one from the intubation kit. Equipment and supplies now lay scattered around, with empty packaging accumulating rapidly. The men looked on in silence until the sound of an approaching siren made them glance up.

'There's the road crew,' Murray said. He checked his watch. 'Took them fifteen minutes.'

George blinked. It had taken the helicopter five minutes to get here. Had they only been on scene for ten minutes? It felt so much longer.

'Got it.' Max's satisfied comment was another surprise. He clamped the needle of the syringe to prevent it advancing any further and George watched the syringe fill with blood before turning back to the monitor.

'VPBs are decreasing,' she reported.

'Let's get another blood pressure and see if we've improved output,' Max instructed. 'Then let's get moving.' Max looked excited. They had a real chance of saving their patient now.

Max was still looking excited when the team arrived back at base well over an hour later. Mike Bingham and Ross White were still working. Wet gear was spread out on a canvas fly sheet out in the sun as they sorted through the contents of a trauma pack.

'What a mess.' George eyed the pile of soggy dressings, batteries and contaminated sterile packs put aside for disposal.

'You're telling me.' Mike was using a towel to dry a blood-pressure cuff. He tightened the valve and tried pumping the bulb. Water oozed from the top and he shook his head in disgust. 'There's water in the gauge. It's useless.'

'Put a fault tag on it and sent it in to Maintenance,' George suggested. 'They might be able to resurrect it.'

Mike grunted, unconvinced. He glanced past George to where Murray and Max were finishing their post-mission check of equipment and supplies. Jack had wandered well away from the helicopter to smoke a cigarette.

'So, how was it? Having a doctor in tow.'

'OK, I guess.' George wasn't about to paint Max's efforts with glowing colours. She didn't want any more enthusiasm on base for a new staff member. Not if it was going to be Max.

Ross added some crêpe bandages to the discard pile. 'Did he take over?' he asked. 'Insist on doing all the interesting procedures himself?'

'Not exactly.' George bit her lip as she saw Murray and Max approaching. Murray was wearing a huge grin.

'You're not going to believe this,' he told his colleagues. 'First time out and Badger here does a pericardiocentesis and saves a life!'

'What?' Both Mike and Ross stood up, their task forgotten. Mike shot George a reproachful glance before turning back to Murray, clearly anticipating further details. George could understand their eager expressions and the reproachful look she had received. She, too, would have been excited at the prospect of hearing about an unusual procedure being performed in the field. Especially one they could recognise the necessity for but were not authorised to carry out themselves.

'Yeah.' Murray was looking like a proud father. 'This chap went down a bank with his farm bike and ended up underneath it with a roll bar smack across his chest. Deteriorated rapidly as soon as the weight was removed.'

George wasn't listening to the account. She was staring at Max. *Badger?* Had he earned his stripes and a nickname *that* quickly? It was an appropriate enough tag, given his unique hair colouring, but the thought that he was already considered a part of the team was disturbing.

'So, how did you know it was a tamponade?' Mike was also staring at Max. 'Jugular vein distention?'

'Beck's triad?' added Ross.

Max nodded. 'Muffled heart sounds, narrow pulse pressure, tachycardia with ventricular arrhythmias. Falling BP out of proportion to blood loss.'

'No signs of major abdominal bleeding,' Murray put in.

'And he arrested?' Ross whistled silently.

'We wouldn't have got him anywhere near Emergency unless he'd had the tamponade relieved.' Murray clapped his hand on Max's shoulder. 'And who thought that having a doc on base would make our job less challenging?'

'I couldn't have done anything without your help.' Max was looking at George. 'You were both fantastic.'

George felt the time warp again. She was back in Emergency, having her first conversation with Max after they'd worked on that case together. Funny they should both have been young men with critical and very rare cardiac injuries. Max had admired her skills then and George had felt proud of herself and her career. Now all she wanted to do was tell Max that there were, in fact, more important things in life.

'So…Badger.' Mike's gaze was aimed at Max's hair. Then it dropped and he grinned at Max. 'How different is it doing a pericardiocentesis to a chest decompression for a tension pneumothorax?'

'Different approach for a start,' Max said. 'You go in by the left costosternal angle, just to the left of the xiphoid. You've got to keep the needle at a ninety-degree angle till you're past the sternum, then you angle up towards the left shoulder.'

The loudspeaker on the hangar wall relayed the ringing of the base telephone.

'I'll get it.' George walked away from the three men, who were now discussing the type of ECG changes that a needle contacting the actual heart muscle could produce. She came out again a few minutes later.

'There's a transfer booked in from the West Coast,' she reported to Murray. 'Post-surgical patient that's going off. Pick-up's not for two hours, though. They've taken her back to Theatre to try and stabilise her. They want a medical escort.'

'Shouldn't be a problem.' Murray eyed Max. 'Do you fancy another run?'

Max hesitated, glancing at George who avoided meeting his gaze.

'It's not a problem if you've got other things on,' Murray continued. 'We have a medic on call for this sort of case and there's plenty of time for him to get here.'

'You may as well see what else the job has to offer,' Ross suggested. 'That is, if you're intending to apply for this job.'

Jack had joined the group. He bounced slightly on his heels. 'Are we going somewhere, then?'

'Medical evacuation from the Coast hospital,' Mike told Jack. 'Don't get too excited, Ripper.'

'Who, me?' Jack grinned. 'Shall I go and start her up?'

'No.' Murray shook his head. 'If the trip's confirmed, take-off won't be for another hour.'

Jack looked disappointed. 'Maybe we'll get something else in the meantime.'

'I hope not.' George stretched her back. 'I could use a coffee.'

'Me, too.' Max smiled at George. 'That is, if you're offering.'

'Sure.' George led the way, turning her head after a few steps. 'Mozzie? Do you want a coffee?'

'Would you mind bringing it out?' Murray asked. 'I'd better have a quick look at this mess. What's happened to the BP cuff, Stretch?'

'It's stuffed,' Mike responded succinctly. 'Hey, George? Mine's white—two sugars.'

Max followed George into the small staff-room. He paced around as George collected mugs and took a carton of milk from the fridge. She smiled wryly as she noticed his expression.

'Takes a while to wind down after a mission like that,' she commented. 'Even when it's successful.'

'It was really exciting,' Max admitted. 'I would never have dreamt of doing a procedure like that on a riverbank with no surgical or intensive care back-up. And it *worked*.'

His smile was contagious but George carried on with her task. 'They're not always exciting,' she warned. 'And a lot of rescue attempts aren't successful. A lot of it becomes routine after a while.'

'But never boring.' Max pulled a chair away from the table but didn't sit down. 'Hell, George, I had no idea just what this job really involves. No wonder you wanted it so badly.'

'That was a long time ago,' George said evenly. 'And maybe I was wrong.'

'No. I was wrong,' Max said quietly. 'I should never have tried to stop you, George.

And I was a fool to walk away when you stood your ground.'

'It was a long time ago,' George repeated. 'Sometimes it takes a long time to really see things in perspective. To know what you should have done differently.' She thought of Murray's analogy. 'The direction you should have taken to get you where you really wanted to be.'

The coffee-mugs lay abandoned. The electric jug had boiled and turned itself off. George ignored it. Max was standing between the bench and the window. The light was behind him and his eyes were too dark to be sure of his expression.

'Do you know now, George?' The query was soft. 'Do you know where you really want to be?'

George nodded slowly. 'Yes. I think I do.'

'Me, too.' Max took a step closer. George held her breath. Was Max going to say what she desperately wanted him to say? Or should she just say it first and see what happened?

'I want—' she began, only to be interrupted by the staffroom door flying open. Murray, Ross and Mike trooped in, closely followed by

Jack. Suddenly the small room was crowded and the moment lost irretrievably.

'Coffee's a bit slow, isn't it?' Mike shoved amicably past George to get to the bench. 'Not like you, George.'

'You might have to learn to make coffee for yourself more often,' George countered. 'I'm not going to be around for ever, you know.'

There was a momentary silence as the men exchanged glances. News of Phil Warrington's visit and her agreement to consider the job in town had had an impact. Ross scowled.

'There's too many things changing around here,' he growled. 'I don't like it.'

'What's changing?' Max sounded wary.

'Big George here has been offered a desk job in town,' Mike told him.

'One that she would be very good at,' Mozzie added.

'And we're getting a doctor on base.' Ross picked up his mug and moved away. 'It won't be the same.'

'Badger here might not take the job,' Ross added dejectedly. 'Who knows what the other applicants might be like?'

'If there *are* any other applicants.' George was edged back as Murray handed Max his coffee. 'It's not a job many doctors would be interested in.'

'I think it's pretty interesting,' Max said with a grin. 'So far.'

'It's dangerous,' George said bluntly. 'And it can be exhausting and dirty and frustrating.'

'Hey, don't put him off.' Murray shook his head. 'It's not that bad.'

'I'm not put off that easily,' Max responded. He was looking straight at George. 'Sometimes it's impossible to be put off something if it's what you really want.'

Murray shook his head again. 'You've got a bad dose already,' he said sadly. 'That's one thing you've got to watch out for in this job. It gets into the blood and you end up doing it far longer than you probably should.'

'Like you, Grandpa,' Mike teased. 'How long ago was it that we celebrated Mozzie's fortieth birthday?'

'Can't seem to remember,' Ross grinned. 'Lost in the mists of time.'

Max was ignoring the banter. He was looking at George again. 'What do you think?' he asked quietly. 'Is Murray right?'

George nodded. 'I've carried on longer than I should have,' she admitted. 'I didn't even let a serious injury stop me.'

'I know,' Max told her. 'I read about it.'

'Did you?' George was startled.

'You mean she made international news?' Murray had tuned in to their conversation.

'No. I only just learned about it. Dougal was doing a bit of research. He was thinking about applying for the job on base himself,' Max explained. 'But I think that was enough to put him off.'

'Very wise,' George commented.

'Probably never happen again, of course,' Murray added. The phone rang as he spoke and he moved off to answer it.

Mike, Ross and Jack were engaged in a conversation comparing their own ages, which were all well short of Murray's. Jack was laying plans for his upcoming thirtieth birthday. Max caught George's eye.

'I'm sorry I didn't know about the accident at the time.'

'How could you?' George shrugged. 'There's a lot we don't know about each other now.'

'Maybe we can change that.' Max spoke very quietly. Only George could hear him. 'I'd like a chance to talk to you properly.'

George took a somewhat shaky breath. She was being given the opportunity to start building that bridge. 'I'd like that, too.' She smiled rather shyly. 'I never did show you what I've done with the inside of the house. Why don't you come out after work and take a tour?'

'It's a date.' Max was still smiling at George as Murray rejoined them.

'The trip to the Coast is confirmed. They've brought the pick-up time forward and we'll be leaving in fifteen minutes. If I need to call in a medical escort, I'll have to do it now.'

'I'll come,' Max told him.

George watched Jack tip the remains of his coffee into the sink. He looked keen to get started on the mission and her heart sank. The trip to the West Coast had to cross the Southern Alps. Plenty of scope there for Jack to spice up his day.

'There's a couple of relatives who want to come as well, apparently,' Murray continued. 'Her parents, I think.'

Jack raised his eyebrows. 'We haven't got that much room.'

'There's no need for us both to go, Mozzie, if we've got a medical escort,' George pointed out. 'You could go home early. Or maybe Max should give this one a miss.'

'No, you need a break,' Murray said firmly. 'Put your feet up and have another coffee. No offence, but we need Max more than you this time.'

Max looked disconcerted. 'What time will we get back, do you think?' he asked Murray.

'By six at the latest,' came the reply. 'Is that a problem?'

'No.' Max smiled. 'I've just got a date I wouldn't want to miss.'

'OK.' Murray glanced briefly at George but his thoughts were elsewhere. 'All settled, then?' He checked his watch. 'We'd better get started. Are you happy, George?'

George knew he was referring to her being left out of the mission but that wasn't what she was thinking about as she caught Max's eye fleetingly.

'Oh, yes,' she said softly. 'I'm very happy.'

*   *   *

George stood outside, almost flattened by the rotor wash as she watched the helicopter take off. It hovered for a second or two then moved swiftly westwards. She watched until it was too far away to be anything more than a speck. It would be at least two hours before they returned. When she'd washed the coffee-mugs the men had all discarded in the sink and had tidied the staffroom, she planned to make out the requisition forms for all the fresh supplies the stocktaking had revealed as necessary. Mike and Ross went to finish off their own tasks. The empty pack was now dry and needed restocking.

The office was quiet apart from the odd buzz of static from the radio tuned to the band the helicopter used. George was pleased she was working in here. She would hear the transmission that would inform the communications centre of the crew's arrival and when they were due to depart. Then she would know exactly how long she had to wait to see Max again.

There was so much to show him at the house. All the woodwork on the grand staircase and the panelling in the library that she had painstakingly stripped back and restored. The new fittings in the bathroom upstairs that they had both once loved to hate. There were the stained-glass windows that she'd had made to replace the broken fanlight panes and which were such a good match he probably wouldn't be able to pick them out from the originals. And there was the wonderful old four-poster bed she'd discovered at an auction several years ago that suited the vast master bedroom so perfectly. The thought of showing Max the bed took George's attention away from the requisition forms with devastating finality.

It took the crackle of an impending radio transmission to break the pleasurable train of George's thoughts. She glanced at the wall clock. Surely they couldn't be anywhere near their destination yet?

'Rescue One to Control. We've got...' The transmission disintegrated into loud buzzing.

George waited for the message to be repeated but it was the communications centre that sounded next.

'Control to Rescue One. You're breaking up. Repeat the message, please.'

'Rescue One...' The words were faint and again static obliterated the message.

George held her breath, her eyes fixed on the radio receiver. Control would have to request another repetition. Or they might try another band.

But the next words did not come from the communications centre. They came from the helicopter, presumably somewhere over the Southern Alps. They were even fainter than the last message but their impact was devastating.

Mayday... Mayday...

CHAPTER NINE

'CONTROL to Rescue One. Do you receive?'

The air caught in Georgina Collins's lungs wasn't going anywhere. She began to feel light-headed.

'Control to Rescue One. Come in, please.'

The crackle of static would have been welcome. Anything could have been clutched at as evidence that the radio on board the helicopter was still transmitting. That somebody would speak as soon they had dealt with whatever emergency had arisen.

'Rescue One...Rescue One. Are you receiving?' The voice of the communications officer was young and female. It was also now tinged with desperation. George had no idea how long they would keep trying. She couldn't bear to listen to the messages bouncing back from the absolute silence they were trying to penetrate. Her breath came out slowly. Automatically. Forced out by the movement of her body as she made stiff legs obey her directions.

Mike and Ross were laughing about something. They were about to get into Mike's car and head home to their families to enjoy what remained of their day off. They didn't know about the black silence that hovered somewhere over the mountain range to the west. George could almost see it—a dark mist that blurred the snowy peaks of the Alps.

'What's up, George? You look like you've seen a ghost.'

Had she? Had she seen three ghosts? Jack, Mozzie and…and *Max*?

'George!' Mike was gripping her shoulders. 'What *is* it?'

'Jack sent a mayday call.' Her voice sounded strange. As though someone else was speaking. 'Control hasn't been able to get any response since.'

'Oh, God.' Any hint of laughter in Mike's expression had drained away, along with a lot of colour. 'Come and sit down, George. Ross, get on the phone, mate. Find out what's going on.'

A lot was going on but it seemed to be happening in slow motion. Civil aviation authorities, police and Search and Rescue organisations had all been alerted. Plans were made and then revised. A potential search area was defined and then expanded. Nobody knew why the emergency locator beacon on the aircraft had failed to activate. And who knew precisely what route Jack Burgess might have taken? The helicopter gave him a freedom he was inclined to exploit. 'The Ripper' was a law unto himself.

'He's crashed once before,' Ross reminded them. 'And he walked away without a scratch.'

'He shouldn't have been allowed to keep his licence,' George said stonily. 'He takes risks.'

'He's a brilliant pilot, George,' Mike told her gently. 'It might seem like taking risks but he can handle virtually anything.'

'If they had time to make a mayday call, then it's more likely to be an engine problem,' Ross put in. 'With a wire strike or catastrophic mechanical failure, things would happen way too fast to transmit anything.'

'And if anyone could get a helicopter down safely because of some problem, Ripper could.' Mike squeezed George's shoulder.

It was now over an hour since George had overheard the mayday call and finally things were beginning to happen.

'Search and Rescue is sending a fixed-wing plane in from here to do some spotting,' Ross told George. 'Mike and I are going with them.'

'I'll come, too,' George said decisively.

'No. Wait for Red. He's coming in to take Rescue Two down to the airfield at Springs Junction where they're setting up the Search and Rescue base. You could go down with him.'

George shook her head. She didn't want to wait for Ted Scott or ride in the smaller back-up helicopter the base had available. It would probably take another hour to get Rescue Two checked and fuelled and then make the trip to Springs Junction.

'I'm a trained civil aviation authority observer,' George reminded Ross. 'I want to be part of this.' Her voice caught. 'I *have* to do something.'

Mike and Ross exchanged glances. 'You go with George in the fixed-wing, Snow. I'll come down with Red.'

The small Cessna held four people. George sat in the front with a pilot she knew only vaguely. Ross sat with someone from Search and

Rescue in the back. They got clearance for take-off from the control tower at the airport and were given runway priority. They taxied in front of a massive jumbo jet which had been delayed for the short time it would take them to clear the air space on their direct route towards the Alps. George closed her eyes and tried to relax. She was going to need strength to focus completely on the task ahead of her but it was so hard to control the turbulent sea of emotions she was experiencing in response to the thoughts she couldn't suppress.

Murray Peters's wife, Jan, and his eldest daughter, Sophie, had arrived at the base just as George had been leaving. George had hugged them both—hard—and felt ashamed at her relief in leaving so that she hadn't had to deal with the fear they'd both been exuding. George had too much of that same fear building within herself. Not just for what she would be losing if disaster had befallen her loved friend, Mozzie. She knew precisely how Jan and Sophie felt, facing the horror of losing a man so central to their lives. Jan adored her husband. She had never complained about the risks his job entailed but George knew that she welcomed him home with a silent prayer of thanks at the end of every shift. Jan had told her so once at a Christmas party. If Jan had lost Murray, she would never feel whole again, but at least she would have his children as a source of strength and comfort.

What would George have if she had lost Max? She could never go back to the limbo of the last five years. A time shaded by regrets but not brightly defined by the knowledge she had now. The knowledge that she could never be whole unless Max was a part of her life. He would have been, too. There was nothing acrimonious between them that couldn't have been sorted out. And they would have done that tonight. George had been absolutely certain that Max felt exactly the same way she did. The look from those black eyes when he'd told Murray that he had a date he wouldn't want to miss had told George everything she needed to know. Tonight would have been the start of the rest of their lives...together. The potential void of the rest of George's life without Max was a threatening darkness that she had to desperately hold at bay.

'We're approaching the search area,' the pilot informed his passengers some time later. 'I'll keep our height up while we do a Track Crawl and then we'll go lower and start the first sector on the grid. We're lucky with this weather.'

George made no response to the cheerful comment about the weather. She was already scanning—concentrating on covering her quadrant. The success of an air search depended primarily on the efficiency of the observers and there was a learned technique to scanning effectively. The pilot was doing a Track Crawl first—following what had been decided was the most likely flight path the helicopter would have taken. A lower height would mean smaller objects on the ground would be seen more easily but the ground would also appear to be moving faster and staying focused on the scanning technique was harder. At a higher altitude they would be scanning a wider area and anything as obvious as the bright canary yellow of Rescue One's fuselage, flashes of reflected sunlight from metal or glass or smoke from a burning wreck would be easily spotted.

George had done the intensive three-day course with the Civil Aviation Authority during the time of rehabilitation from her back injury. She had learned the intricacies of the anatomy of eyes and physiological processes of vision. She knew that in order to 'see' anything properly, the human eye had to move by 'saccades'—small series of steps with a brief pause between each step to allow processing of the information received. She knew about the blind spot caused by the position of the optic nerve in the retina, where one eye could miss seeing an object completely, and how to combat the problem by moving her head as well as her eyes.

George also knew to combat glare which was why she was wearing her flight helmet with its tinted visor. She knew to reduce fatigue by totally refocussing her eyes periodically by looking at the aircraft's wing instead of the ground. She knew how to judge the distance from the aircraft and keep her scanning to half the track spacing of four kilometres. George knew enough to be confident that she was doing this job to the best of her ability. She knew that the others were doing the same but the minutes ticked past with no hint of success.

There were some false alarms, such as when Ross spotted some trampers on a track which could well have been the one Dougal and Max had used until Dougal's accident. They circled for a closer look and the trampers waved to let them know they were fine. George felt an unreasonable spurt of anger at their cheerful response. Then the anger changed direction with shocking focus. How *could* Max have put himself in this position in the first place? There had been no good reason for this sudden interest in helicopters. He had a brilliant career. He couldn't afford to take a long time out from work as an emergency consultant. Advances in the field were being made all the time and he would lose both knowledge and skills by a prolonged absence. George felt furious with Max for even courting the remote danger that a ride in a helicopter represented.

And yet it was her fault. The only reason for Max to have developed this interest was because it was associated with her. Was Max simply trying to prove that he was sincere in believing he shouldn't have tried to interfere with her career ambitions or opportunities? Was he becoming involved because understanding how she felt about her work might bring them closer together? If so, it hadn't been necessary. George would have told him how insignificant any of it now seemed in comparison to the way she felt about him. Now she might never have the chance to say anything to Max ever again.

George blinked tightly and bit her lip hard enough to draw blood. Vision blurred by tears and a mind racing along dark pathways were the last things she could afford right now. They were working tracks through defined sectors of the search area at a reduced altitude now. It took about ten minutes to complete each sector. Another plane was being brought in. Thanks to Jack's lenient attitude to direct routes, there were too many sectors to be covered by one aircraft in the remaining daylight available.

After nearly two hours in the air, the Cessna was diverted the short distance to the rural airstrip at Springs Junction. The runway was grass and the small mob of sheep used to control the growth were well adapted to staying clear of landing aircraft. The animals were congregated in the furthermost corner of the airfield at present, clearly overawed by the extraordinary amount of activity disturbing their customary peace. The Cessna brought the number of small planes up to three. Rescue Two was parked near the corrugated-iron hangar. Several four-wheel-drive vehicles and cars flanked the tiny shed that served as a control tower and terminal building. Most of the people were inside the hangar but George and Ross were sent to the shed. Coffee and food were waiting for them.

George wasn't remotely hungry but forced herself to eat a cheese sandwich. Hunger, as well as fatigue, could undermine the ability to observe and she had every intention of getting airborne again as soon as the Cessna had been refuelled. She swallowed the painful lumps the sandwich made with copious amounts of coffee. As a local farmer's wife refilled her cup she heard the sound of one of the other small planes taking off. Then a very noisy new one came in to land.

'That'll be Fred,' the woman told George. 'My husband. He runs a top-dressing outfit. He said he'd be here as soon as he could.' Satisfied that her family were doing all they could to help, the woman nodded. She picked up a tray of buttered scones and moved towards the door that joined the shed to the hangar. George followed.

Ordnance survey maps were spread over an enormous wall board at the back of the hangar, overlapped and pinned into place to cover the whole search area accurately. Colour-coded pins marked sectors and some were flagged to indicate having been searched once already. Conversations between Search and Rescue officials and the pilots were calm and George felt slightly reassured by the businesslike and thorough attention to detail.

Ted Scott broke off his conversation as soon as he spotted George. In no time at all she was folded in his arms and it was only then that George allowed the reality of what was happening to hit home. Only Ted was aware of her shaking body and the stifled sobs. He led her quickly outside, encouraged her to talk privately and made comforting sounds as he accepted the wave of fear and grief that George couldn't hold back any longer.

'I just can't believe this is happening.' George finally calmed herself enough to wipe her eyes and blow her nose on the handkerchief Ted produced from the pocket of his overalls. 'I just wish it had been me on that trip instead of Mozzie.'

Ted shook his head but George nodded. At least that way she and Max would have been together. For ever.

Ted put his arm around George's shoulders. 'We don't know that we've lost them, yet. Jack's survived a crash before, remember.'

'Not in the mountains.' George cast her gaze at the unforgiving landscape surrounding the airfield. 'We're going to run out of daylight. If any of them are alive and badly injured they'll never survive a night in the open.' Her gaze caught the helicopter Ted had flown in. 'Are you going to join the search? Are your ears OK?'

'They're fine.'

'Come on, then.' George stepped away from the comforting weight of Ted's arm. 'We'll get them to assign a new sector to you and I'll come as observer.'

Ted shook his head. 'I'm on hold for a bit. There's still quite a lot of good flying time in this weather. It won't be too dark before 9 p.m. I need a winch operator and winch crew to stay with me—in case we need to check a sighting.'

George swallowed hard. If a crash had occurred in even a relatively inaccessible area, the quickest way to ascertain whether there were any survivors and whether there was any point in despatching further rescue efforts was to winch somebody down. It was a grim task that George had had to do herself in the past.

'We've got an army helicopter on standby if we need it,' Ted continued. 'Mike and Ross will come with me.'

'No. Let me—please,' George begged. 'Ross can go back up in the Cessna.'

'Not a good idea, George.'

'Why not?'

'You're too affected by this. Too close.'

'And you're not? And Mike and Ross—do you think they're feeling detached and professional about this?' George's voice rose passionately. 'For heaven's sake, Ted. These people are our friends. Our colleagues. And Max, the doctor on board, he's my... Was my...' George trailed into silence. She hoped Ted could read in her face how important this was. Catching his arm, George spoke more quietly. 'I may never go up in a helicopter again, Ted. Please, let me do this.'

The grip she had on his arm was fierce. Her hands were no longer shaking. Ted recognised the look of sheer determination on George's face and he saw something else as well. Something he'd only ever seen in his wife's face. An emotion he didn't want to try and analyse right now because he was afraid for George. Ted nodded, slowly.

'OK, George. You can come.'

They walked back to the hangar, arm in arm, to find Mike striding out to meet them. His face was grim.

'They've located the crash site,' he told them quietly.

George and Ted stopped as suddenly as if faced by a solid wall. They waited but Mike looked away, muscles bunching tensely at the sides of his jaw.

'And?' Ted's prompt was gentle but uncompromising.

Mike Bingham swallowed painfully. George could see the effort in the way his Adam's apple jerked up and then took such a long time to return.

'And there's no sign of life.'

CHAPTER TEN

NO SIGN of life.

The numbness spread with remarkable rapidity, having started like a stone landing in the pit of her stomach on hearing Mike Bingham's chilling statement. The feeling spread throughout Georgina Collins's body. No sign of life. Her legs felt like the bones were turning to stone as George started the walk towards the small red helicopter. This was going to be the longest walk of her life. Ted Scott had time for a brief but urgent conversation with Mike before the two men caught up with her.

'Are you sure you want to do this, George?'

'Yes.'

Ted and Mike exchanged a long glance. Ted cleared his throat and spoke gruffly. 'Let's do it, then.'

No unnecessary words were spoken during the preparation for the flight. George put the harness on herself before any discussion could

257

take place over whether she or Mike would operate the winch or be the one lowered to the scene. Mike strapped himself into the winch operator's seat without voicing any opinion. The flight was brief although the site was well away from the area that the Cessna had been scanning earlier.

'Target 9 o'clock, 600 metres.'

Ted circled the area with a wide circumference. George stared straight ahead. She couldn't look. Not quite yet.

'Potential landing spot,' Ted observed. 'How far from the target will it be?'

'At least an hour's walk—and there's no sign of any tracks.'

'No good, then.' The helicopter moved out of its hover. 'Turning downwind.'

Mike flicked a switch on the control panel beside him. 'Checking winch power.'

George waited. There was nothing she needed to do just yet and it really didn't matter how quickly or slowly events unfolded. She had lost control over her life. There was nothing she could do but go with the flow and bless the numbness that cushioned her soul.

'Turning base leg.'

'Roger.' George could feel Mike's glance. He wasn't happy about this. Her colleagues wanted to protect her but they all knew there was no real emotional safety zone available. George's fingers fumbled as she checked her harness and seat belt.

'Three hundred metres.'

'OK, George?' Mike's tone begged reassurance. George met his gaze steadily and nodded.

'Speed back. Clear door.'

George could see the treetops bending in the rotor wash. She couldn't yet see anything on the ground. How widely spread was the wreckage? Had there been an explosion on impact... Or a later fire to char the cheerful canary yellow of the fuselage?

'Door back and locked. Bringing hook inboard.'

George attached the hook to her harness. She felt unnaturally calm. This time she knew there would be no hint of the usual fear a winching procedure could evoke. She had nothing left to fear in life. The worst had already happened. Her body moved automatically. George turned and positioned herself on the skids. Looking down to one side of her feet, she caught a glimpse of bright yellow.

'Eighty metres,' Mike stated evenly. 'Seventy...sixty... Clear to boom out.'

'Clear.'

'Booming out... Boomed out.'

George was still looking down. It was more than a glimpse of yellow. A lot more. Rescue One lay upside down, its skids directly below her. The clear bubble of the cockpit was shattered, the metal of the body crumpled, the rotors twisted and bent, but the machine was clearly recognisable.

'Clear to winch.'

'Clear.' A moment's silence from Ted and then he spoke quietly. 'Take care, George.'

George watched the ground coming closer. Would the crew still be strapped into their seats in what remained of Rescue One? Equipment had been scattered. An oxygen cylinder lay well away, at the start of the skid track where the helicopter had made first contact with the ground. The scrub had been flattened. A trauma pack lay further up the gouged track, its contents spilling onto the rocky soil.

'Minus ten,' George warned Mike. The winching slowed as George counted off the distance between her feet and the ground. 'Five…four…three…' George bent her knees to absorb the contact, then straightened and un-hooked herself. She held the hook clear and gave Mike the thumbs-up signal. Rescue Two moved away a little. The radio stayed silent. The crew would be waiting for George to make first contact. Despite the relatively intact appearance of the crashed helicopter, nobody was expecting a miracle.

A treetrunk nearby was deeply scarred, the branches on one side ripped clear or dangling like badly broken limbs. A large, smooth boul-der amongst the scrub was streaked with bright yellow paint. The mangled undergrowth caught at George's legs as she made her way closer to the wreckage. She could hear nothing over the sound of Rescue Two, hovering to-wards her right. George could sense the steady attention she was under from both Ted and Mike.

The side door of Rescue One was closed and crumpled. There was no chance of entry or even seeing inside thanks to the scrub that covered the windows. George edged through the archway that a bent rotor had formed, its tip buried deeply in the soil. The front of the helicopter was open, the pilot still firmly strapped to his seat. Jack was dead. George knew that well before she stripped off a glove to lay her hand on his neck. The action was partly protocol and partly self-protection. She wanted to buy just a little more time before looking into the interior of the machine.

George frowned as she tried to think logically. Murray had been sitting up front beside Jack when they left the base, leaving Max alone in the rear of the helicopter. There was blood on the front passenger seat but the seat belt was still attached and looked undamaged. Had Murray changed position to sit in the back or had he been somehow thrown clear?

Max must have also been ejected by the impact because there was no sign of either of the men. George stopped herself contacting Ted. She needed more information. There was no urgency in instigating an operation for body retrieval but she had to ascertain that that was all that was going to be needed. George moved back out of the wreckage carefully. She scanned what she could see of the surrounding area. Trees loomed close on her left, the scrub opened to rocks marking a steep slope away to her right. She could see no hint of the orange flight suits that both Mozzie and Max had been wearing.

'George?' The radio crackled into life inside her helmet. The suspense was too much for Ted and Mike.

'Jack's dead,' George relayed calmly. 'I'm still looking for the others.'

'Check the brush edging the fuselage.' Ted suggested tightly. 'They may be underneath.'

George pulled at small branches, fighting her way around the large machine, more than half expecting to see a foot or hand to be visible after Ted's horrific suggestion.

'Nothing,' she reported minutes later. 'I'm going to check further back.'

'George?'

'Can you repeat?' George listened hard. 'You're very faint. Did you say something, Ted?'

Ted's voice was clear now. 'Negative,' he responded. 'I wasn't transmitting, George.'

'George!'

Her head turned with painful swiftness. The call of her name had been faint because it hadn't been a radio transmission. A figure in orange overalls was standing, leaning against the trunk of a tree. George pulled her helmet off as she pushed past a larger shrub and scrambled over the boulder with the yellow paint streaks. Without the tinted visor she might be able to tell whether it was Mozzie…or…

Max.

It *was* Max. He was alive. Standing. His face was cut, one eye was swollen almost shut and the streak of white hair obscured by what looked like dried blood. George dropped her heavy leather gloves, reaching up to touch his face.

'I'm all right.'

George stared at him, her hand still touching Max's cheek, absorbing the sound of his voice. The numbness was still there. Her mind was unwilling to trust the information her senses were gathering.

'I'm all right,' Max repeated. 'I'm alive, George. And so is Murray.'

The numbness left her then, the new sensation agonising in its intensity. Then they were in each other's arms, their embrace fierce enough to add physical pain to the emotional overload.

'Careful,' Max grunted reluctantly. 'I've got a few bruises.' He held George for only a moment longer. 'Murray's hurt, George. I've done what I can but he needs to get out of here. And Jack's dead.'

'I know.' George sucked in air. She hadn't been expecting this. Mozzie needed her help. George had always done her best for every patient that had needed her as a paramedic. This time she was going to do more than her best. 'How bad is Mozzie?'

'Pretty shocked. He was able to walk after the crash—he wanted us to get clear fast in case of a fire.' Max was holding George's arm, leading her behind the tree he had been leaning against. 'He's got an open pneumothorax which I've covered. He's also got abdominal bleeding. I went back for the trauma pack. I've started an IV and we're onto the second unit of saline, but his BP's still dropping.'

George knelt beside Murray. An occlusive dressing was over the wound in his chest, taped on three sides to allow air to escape but nothing to be sucked in as he breathed. His respiration rate was rapid and the efforts shallow. His abdomen was distended and George could feel the rigidity over the left side. Murray's eyes opened as he felt George's touch.

'Hey—Big George!' Murray was smiling faintly. ''Bout time you showed up.'

'Bit of a beer gut you've got here, mate.' George masked her anxiety but their eye contact belied her light-hearted tone. Murray was seriously injured and they both knew it.

'What the hell.' Murray's lips twisted wryly. 'Who needs a spleen, anyway?'

George bent closer. 'I'm going to get you out of here, Mozzie. I'll get Mike to send down the stretcher.' She looked at Max. 'Will you be able to help me carry him?'

'Sure.'

George's eyes raked Max rapidly. He looked pale. The swelling around his eye was increasing. 'Were you knocked out?'

'No.'

Murray reached up to touch George. 'This wasn't Jack's fault, George. He was brilliant. Found a clear space and almost got us down in one piece.'

'Something went wrong with the engines,' Max added. 'One failed and then the other was cutting out. Jack said something about fuel lines.'

George was still examining Max visually. 'What's wrong with your wrist?'

'Just a sprain. I'm all right, George.' Max returned her intent stare. 'Just get on with what you need to do for Mozzie.'

George unclipped her hand-held radio from her belt and turned it on. 'Rescue Two, how do you read?'

'Hell, George,' Ted's voice exploded from the radio. 'We've been trying to contact you.' He sounded irate. 'You should have your radio on at all times. We couldn't see you in the trees. What the hell's going on down there?'

'We need a stretcher,' George told him calmly. 'Mozzie is Status 2, with chest and abdominal injuries. Max is Status 3.'

'Do you want the trauma pack sent down?' Mike sounded excited.

'Negative. Max has already started an IV. We're ready to roll.'

The stretcher had been winched down by the time George had scrambled back to the clearer area. Despite a swollen and obviously painful wrist injury, Max helped George secure Murray to the stretcher and carry him to the winching site. It took only minutes to get him up and loaded into Rescue Two. There was no chance of winching Max clear yet. Rescue Two was too small to take any more passengers or patients and Murray needed to get to hospital as quickly as possible.

'I'm going back down,' George informed her colleagues. 'I'll wait with Max until you guys get back or someone else comes.' She positioned herself on the skids. 'Get me down again, Stretch, and then take good care of Mozzie.'

'Roger.' Mike flicked her a grin. 'Clear to boom out, Red?'

'Got a survival pack, George? Might be a while before you get out.'

'I've got it.' George was smiling. 'Don't worry. It won't be the first time you've left me behind.'

'That's what I'm worried about. You're making a habit of this, George.' Ted's tone quickly became businesslike. 'Clear to boom out, Stretch.'

'Roger.' Mike was moving fast.

George took one last look at Mozzie before stepping off the skids. He was watching her and held up one hand, with his thumb pointing up. George returned the signal.

'Clear to winch.' Mike was looking down at George now.

'Clear,' Ted confirmed.

The descent was smooth. George had her feet on the ground again in what seemed like no time at all. The winch cable was swiftly retracted and Rescue Two moved away at speed. For the second time in almost the same number of weeks, George found herself isolated on the top of a mountain.

With Max.

'Take the flight suit off.'

'Why?'

'Because I intend to check your injuries.'

'I told you I'm all right.'

George gave Max a very level stare. 'Right now you're my professional responsibility. You've been through a major traumatic event and you have some injuries that are obvious. You may well have others that you're not even aware of yourself yet. Your flight suit is shredded down the back and I need to check your back and chest and listen to your breathing.' George spoke firmly, allowing Max no opportunity to protest. 'I'm doing my job here, Max. I'd appreciate it if you would co-operate.'

Max grinned. 'You do that very well.'

'Do what?'

'Tell people off.'

'Get on with it, Max.' George was fishing a stethoscope out of the fresh trauma pack she had brought down with her. 'I'm not in the mood for an argument.'

'I can tell.' Max was still smiling as he unzipped the orange overalls. He winced as he slowly pulled his arms free of the sleeves.

'What hurts?' George queried sharply.

'Just my wrist.'

'I'll check that in a minute. Your chest and head are my first priorities. Turn around.'

It wasn't just the flight suit that had been damaged. The jersey Max had been wearing underneath was also badly torn. Blood stained the shirt beneath the jersey but the laceration was superficial.

'I'm afraid you've ruined your nice jersey.' George tried not to sound as absurdly pleased as she felt. 'It's the one Raewyn knitted for you, isn't it?'

'Rowena,' Max corrected. His voice sounded a bit muffled as George fitted the stethoscope to her ears. 'I never liked it much anyway. Too fussy.'

George didn't have to suppress the small smile that curled the corners of her mouth. Max couldn't see her as she stood behind him. She placed the disc of the stethoscope against his back. 'Take a deep breath, Max.'

Satisfied that there were no injuries that could affect Max's breathing, George moved quickly to assess his head injury. 'Are you sure you weren't KO'd?'

'Absolutely. I remember everything.' Max's head turned beneath George's fingers. Now sitting in a sheltered pocket behind the large boulder, what remained of the helicopter was out of sight but George knew that that was what Max could see just now.

'Was it instant?' she asked quietly. 'For Jack?'

'Yes.' Max was silent for a moment. 'He was a real hero, George. In control right up to the last moment—until we hit that tree. We really thought he could pull it off.' Max's voice was ragged. 'I'm very sorry he didn't.'

'So am I.' George continued her examination solemnly. Max answered her questions and followed the directions she gave while checking the strength and mobility of his limbs. Happy that she hadn't missed anything, George dressed the wound on Max's forehead and then returned to the swollen left wrist.

'I don't think it's broken. Your limb baselines are fine and you've got a full range of movement even though it's painful. I'll splint it until it's X-rayed, though.'

'OK.' Max sat silently as George bandaged his wrist to the splint. Having applied the alligator clip to fasten the bandage, she looked up, catching Max's gaze.

'At least this will have put you off a job with rescue helicopters.'

'Certainly a trial by fire,' Max agreed.

'You can't mean you're still thinking about it?' George sat back on her heels with a horrified expression.

'Well, the odds of something like this happening again must be astronomical. People might consider it a good insurance policy to have me on board from now on.'

George narrowed her eyes. 'There's a dead man lying over there. A colleague of mine. He's only twenty-nine years old,' she said angrily. 'I can't believe you're making jokes about this.'

'Perhaps I'm not joking.' Max was meeting George's glare without blinking. 'You came a lot closer than I did to being killed by this job.'

'I would have given it up then if I'd had any sense.'

'Why didn't you, then? You're not exactly unintelligent, George. You've got more than enough sense.'

George looked away. 'Maybe I had nothing to stop *for*.'

Max spoke softly. 'Maybe I don't either.'

'Don't be ridiculous,' George snapped. 'You're a consultant emergency physician.

You're heading for the peak of a brilliant career.'

'I'm nearly forty, George.' Max leaned back against the boulder and gazed towards the trees. 'I expect I'm entitled to consider having a mid-life crisis. Isn't that the traditional time to re-evaluate what you're doing with your life? What you want from the future?'

'This job is *not* what you want.'

'It might be.'

George expelled her breath in an angry huff. 'I'll make sure you don't get it, then.'

'How will you do that?' Max sounded curious.

'I know people.' George was offhand. 'They'll listen to what I say. I'll tell them you're not suitable.'

'Why am I not suitable?' Max was indignant now.

'Because you're stupid.'

Max's jaw sagged. 'Excuse me?'

George glared at him again. Now that her role as a paramedic was no longer needed, personal issues were forcing themselves to the surface. The emotional wringer she had been through in the last few hours had exhausted any reserves of strength. 'You've just been lucky enough to survive a disaster that's killed one person and seriously injured another,' she informed Max coldly. 'And you're too stupid to realise what that means.' A painful lump was forming in her throat. 'This is a dangerous profession. You could have been killed.' George couldn't control the sudden tremble of her lips. 'Doesn't that bother you? Just a little bit?'

'It bothers me quite a lot.' Max was observing George closely. 'The question is, why does it bother *you*?'

'Why do you *think* it bothers me?' George shot back with exasperation.

'No.' Max shook his head. 'I'm asking you. I want you to tell me why you're so angry.'

George stared at her clenched fists. 'I'm angry because you put yourself into a dangerous position for no good reason. You didn't give a toss who might be affected if something happened to you.'

'Like who?'

'Like the people who care about you.'

During the short silence that followed, Max shifted his position, moving away from the boulder and onto his knees. He was now much closer to where George sat, miserably hunched. Reaching out, he caught her chin and tilted her head so that she was forced to look up at him.

'Do you care about me, George?' Max asked softly.

'Of course I do, you idiot.' George sniffed as tears became imminent. 'I love you…I always have.' Her breath caught and almost strangled her next words. 'I didn't realise how much until I saw you again and recognised how empty my life has been since you left.'

Max's hand left George's chin. He stroked the tears from her cheeks and then smoothed the hair back from her forehead. 'I love you, too,' he said slowly. 'And I feel exactly the same way. We should never have lost each other.' His hand stilled and a wry smile curled one corner of his mouth. 'The reason we did is because I did just what you're trying to do right now.'

George pulled sharply away from Max's hand. 'What?'

Max gazed at her steadily. 'You're trying to stop me doing something I want to do.

Something I might need to do to prove to myself that I *can* do it—even if it's difficult and dangerous and not something that someone like me would be expected to want to do.'

'You can't be serious.' George was incredulous. 'You can't really want to work on the base.'

'No.' Max looked away for a moment. He let out a long breath and then smiled at George almost wistfully. 'Maybe I've been playing with the idea just enough to recognise how it *could* be like that. It could become a challenge that had to be met because it would make a statement about who I was and what I was capable of doing. If I *did* feel like that, it wouldn't be right for you to try and stop me.'

Max was talking about himself, George realised. Confessing his error in trying to stop her all those years ago. And suddenly she thought she could see his side.

'I would only try and stop you because it's dangerous. Because I would be too afraid of losing you.' George bit her lip. 'Do you have any idea what it was like for me on that search plane? Looking and looking for you and thinking you might be dead?' George was unaware of the fresh tears that rolled down her face. 'Wondering how the hell I could face the rest of my life if you weren't there to be a part of it?'

Max pulled George into his arms and held her close. 'I've got a very good idea,' he told her gently. 'It would be exactly the same way I felt that night you came home with a black eye. Or the day I heard about the ambulance officer killed at the scene of that motorway accident. Or the nights I lay awake wondering how I could cope with that fear if I knew you were flying around in helicopters every day.' Max rested his head against George's as he held her even closer. 'It's a bloody dangerous job, you know.'

'I know,' George agreed quietly. 'And I'm not going to do it any more.'

'Neither am I.'

George moved so that she could return the smile she heard in Max's voice. 'I know who I am now, Max,' she said earnestly. 'I don't *have* to be one of the boys any longer.' She smiled shyly. 'I think I quite like being a woman.'

Max leaned forward and placed a lingering kiss on George's lips. 'That's good. Because I quite like you being a woman as well.'

'If I wasn't a woman then I could never have the chance to meet another challenge. One that I want to meet very much. But I won't if you don't want me to.' George chewed her lip tentatively. 'You get as much say in this one as I do.'

'Oh, no!' Max groaned. 'What is it—a new job?'

'You could say that.'

'Is it dangerous?'

'It has its share of dangers, I guess.' George looked thoughtful. 'It's also exciting and challenging and very rewarding, but it's a long-term career.'

Max sighed with slightly overdone tolerance. A ghost of a smile made his lips twitch. 'What is it this time? A top-dressing pilot? Submarine crew member? An astronaut? What do you want to be now, George?'

'A mother.'

Max absorbed her statement slowly. He looked extremely serious. 'I hope it's my baby that's going to allow you to achieve this ambition.'

'I wouldn't want anybody else's.'

'That means it's a joint appointment,' Max said thoughtfully. 'We both need the right qualifications for this job.'

George was trying not to smile. 'Would you like to interview me?'

'You bet.' Max settled back against the boulder again, pulling George with him so that she nestled in his arms. 'Why do you want this job, Ms Collins?'

George wriggled free. She held Max's face between her hands and leaned close. 'Because I am totally and absolutely in love with the man who will be the father of my baby. Even if I never had children I would want to spend the rest of my life with him—wherever he wanted to be.'

'Wherever?'

George nodded.

'Would you consider a small farm just out of town? A huge old house that might need a lot of work? I can't say how much because nobody's let me see inside for a very long time.' Max kissed George again. 'And there's a downside to the place. A goat who tries to send people into orbit and a donkey who eats anything—including jeans.'

George was laughing. 'You want to live here? In Christchurch?' Her dark blue eyes shone excitedly.

'This is my interview,' Max said sternly. 'I get to ask the questions. Is that where you'd like to live?'

'I want to be with you, Max. It doesn't matter where it is.'

'OK.' Max was brisk. 'I've made a decision.'

'And?'

'You've got the job. Now it's your turn.'

'I think I might have to wait for my turn.' George was watching a speck on the horizon. It grew rapidly into a large, grey shape. She could hear the sound of the rotors on the army helicopter. Suddenly their surroundings leapt back into focus. Together, they had managed to transport themselves miles away from the reality of the crash scene. Focussing on each other, they had even managed to put aside the tragic fact of Jack's body lying nearby. How astonishing, George thought, to have found such joy in a situation like this. But the joyful prospect of a future together would have to be left for the moment. For a while at least, they would have to concentrate on other things.

George's turn to conduct an interview was delayed by several hours. Max was taken away for X-rays and treatment as soon as they arrived at Christchurch hospital. George was with Jan Peters, providing encouragement and reassurance as they waited for Murray to come out of the recovery room after his lengthy session in the operating theatre. She stayed until Jan had had some private time with Murray after he'd been transferred into the intensive care unit.

'He wants to see you,' she told George with a smile.

Murray was still very drowsy. George inspected the bedside monitors as she took hold of his hand. 'They were telling us the truth,' she said happily. 'You're going to be just fine.'

'What about Jack? Have they brought him out?'

George nodded. 'Phil Warrington has contacted his family. They want us to arrange the funeral. They said this job was his life. They want his ashes scattered on the mountains from a helicopter.'

Murray closed his eyes. 'Don't let that happen to you, Big George. There's more to life than helicopters.'

'I know.' George squeezed his hand. 'I'm getting out now, Mozzie.'

'Good.' Murray's eyes opened again. 'And Badger? Is he OK?'

'Max is fine. He won't be taking a job at the base, though.'

Murray nodded faintly. 'I'm not surprised. Bit offputting.'

'It's not that,' George explained. 'I think he might be going to get a better job offer any time now.'

The interview with Max was brief. George found him sitting on a bed in the emergency department, talking to Dougal. Max's face clouded anxiously as he caught sight of George.

'How's Mozzie?'

'Stable. They removed his spleen and sorted out the chest wound. He's going to be OK.'

'Thank goodness for that.'

George eyed the fresh bandage on Max's wrist and the neat stitches that had closed the wound on his forehead. 'Someone's patched you up nicely.'

'I'm fine. Just a bit tired.'

'Time to go home, then,' Dougal suggested. 'I'll call a taxi for us, mate.'

'Actually, I've got something else I need to do. You'd better go on without me.' Max looked at Dougal pointedly. 'Thanks for coming in.'

'No problem. I'll wait for you, mate.'

'No, you don't need to.' Max said firmly. 'Go home, Dougal.'

'But—'

'I'll see that Max gets home, Dougal.' George decided it was time to spell out to Dougal that his company was superfluous right now. 'I just need to have a quick word with him.'

'Oh.' Dougal looked at George, then at Max, before returning his gaze to George. 'Oh-h!' He said delightedly. He reached for his crutches and then winked at George. 'I'm gone,' he said, grinning broadly. 'In fact, I was never here.'

George pulled the curtain of the cubicle shut as soon as Dougal had moved away. Then she climbed onto the bed beside Max.

'About that new job,' she began. 'Why do you want it, Max?'

He smiled. 'Probably because I'm totally and absolutely in love with the woman who will be the mother of my baby. I want to marry her and relish every moment we get to spend together for the rest of our lives.'

George slid off the bed and held out her hand to Max. 'You've got the job,' she informed him solemnly. 'When would you like to start?'

Max took the outstretched hand and pulled George towards him. 'Right now,' he said softly. 'When would you like to start yours?'

George let go of his hand and stood on tip-toe to wind her arms around Max's neck. 'Right now sounds good to me.'

'Hey!' Max pulled back just before their lips met. 'What's the time?'

'Nearly 10 p.m. Why?'

'I'm late. I had a date I didn't want to miss tonight. A house I really wanted to see.'

George laughed softly. 'Come on, then. I'll take you home with me.'

Max grinned broadly as he swung his legs over the side of the bed. 'Sounds good to me. I just hope you can cope with a long date.'

'How long did you have in mind?'

'How 'bout the rest of your life?'

George was locked into the tender gaze Max was giving her. She took a long, long breath, revelling in the pure joy she felt. Then she smiled.

'Sounds good to me, Max,' she whispered. 'Very, very good.'

MEDICAL ROMANCE™

Large Print

Titles for the next six months...

August

GUILTY SECRET	Josie Metcalfe
PARTNERS BY CONTRACT	Kim Lawrence
MORGAN'S SON	Jennifer Taylor
A VERY TENDER PRACTICE	Laura MacDonald

September

INNOCENT SECRET	Josie Metcalfe
HER DR WRIGHT	Meredith Webber
THE SURGEON'S LOVE-CHILD	Lilian Darcy
BACK IN HER BED	Carol Wood

October

A WOMAN WORTH WAITING FOR	Meredith Webber
A NURSE'S COURAGE	Jessica Matthews
THE GREEK SURGEON	Margaret Barker
DOCTOR IN NEED	Margaret O'Neill

MILLS & BOON®

MEDICAL ROMANCE™

Large Print

November

THE DOCTORS' BABY	Marion Lennox
LIFE SUPPORT	Jennifer Taylor
RIVALS IN PRACTICE	Alison Roberts
EMERGENCY RESCUE	Abigail Gordon

December

A VERY SINGLE WOMAN	Caroline Anderson
THE STRANGER'S SECRET	Maggie Kingsley
HER PARTNER'S PASSION	Carol Wood
THE OUTBACK MATCH	Lucy Clark

January

EMERGENCY GROOM	Josie Metcalfe
THE MARRIAGE GAMBLE	Meredith Webber
HIS BROTHER'S SON	Jennifer Taylor
THE DOCTOR'S MISTRESS	Lilian Darcy

MILLS & BOON®

0702 LP 2P P2 Medical